All

we know

of heaven

St.
martin's press
NEW YORK

All
we know
of heaven

ANNA TUTTLE VILLEGAS

Book Design by Gretchen Achilles

ISBN 0-312-14613-2

First Edition: February 1997

10   9   8   7   6   5   4   3   2   1

With gratitude to
Emily Dickinson;
Doris Michaels, for her faith in the manuscript from Lodi;
Tom and Sandra McCormack, the consummate editors;
and Addie, my daughter and my muse.

Contents

The Heart asks Pleasure—first—
And then—Excuse from Pain—
And then—those little Anodynes
That deaden suffering—

And then—to go to sleep—
And then—if it should be
The will of its Inquisitor
The privilege to die—

Emily Dickinson, 1862

CHAPTER ONE

Love reckons by itself—alone

ॐ

Love reckons by itself—alone—
"As large as I"—relate the Sun
To One who never felt it blaze—
Itself is all the like it has—

EMILY DICKINSON 1864

ON THE EDGE of my town, where seedy marigolds sprout from bald tractor tires and the stucco and brick facades give way to chapped clapboard, I see that Hank Rodriguez has pulled down the dying cottonwood as he had promised. In its place grows a sturdy fruitless plum just done with showering its petals, one uplifted branch dangling a blue and gold paper kite. Good match.

On the five-acre parcel that Hedy and Tom Swanson selected, two fat pinto ponies are grazing on the front lawn, so freshly cut that the mower tracks band the wet grass, and the ponies' tiny hooves leave a dented trail of half-moons. The twins have left the gate open again. Good match.

In town, where subdivision sprawl is denied by the graceful lay-out of the broad old streets, Trevor Tuskes has transformed his postage stamp of a front yard into a vegetable plot. After the final frost of our late winter, I saw him sitting on the ground, one arthritic hand turning the damp loam with a butcher knife. Now the tomato vines bear star-shaped yellow blossoms. Next month, the hard green globes will promise a feast. I know if I stop by in August, Trevor will thrust a bag of sleek red fruit into my hands. Good match.

I cherish the lasting fit between a deserving buyer and a home of character. For years after I have closed a sale, I drive past old listings to study the revisions rendered by their occupants, the inheritors of my artwork. Have I companioned well the buyers with their homes? I want to know. Whose children have grown so numerous that the house needs remodeling? Who has given up on the endless summer mowing and turned his front yard into a rock-lined riverbed? Whose misfortunes are flagged by the traitorous FOR SALE signs of another realtor?

Selling houses is a delicate art.

I practice it well, better than I do most things. I appreciate the language of the trade, the symbolism inherent in the marriage of a person to a dwelling. I like to read people and to mate them with walls that speak their personalities. I pride myself on my craft: the ascending arrangement of possibilities, a quick eye that catches a buyer's preference for small rooms over large, the intuitive murmur of an understated adjective—all of which require the gentle choreography of a matchmaker, a matchmaker who isn't pressed for time.

The Walters are not a good match for the Leland House. I know this the moment Tammy Walters squeals.

"Not a bearing wall," Phil Walters grunts from his knees, where he has lowered his considerable bulk to pry away the 1950s wallboard from what is to remain, rightfully and eternally, I swear to myself, a pantry wall.

"Hon," Tammy stoops to croon into her husband's lowered ear "if it's not a bearing wall that means we could tear it out and do a kitchen nook!"

She turns to wink at me through permed bangs.

"Didn't you always want a kitchen nook? I have always dreamed of living in a house with a kitchen nook!"

"Lovely," I say, turning away from the upended corduroy of Phil's rear and the even more gruesome vision of nightmarish wallpaper flocked with dozens and dozens of beribboned geese. My favorite listing? Desecrated by a kitchen nook? As I move out of earshot from the kitchen to the original parlor, I mutter under my breath what I will later shout to Zoey in the safety of my office: only a cretin would turn a perfectly usable walk-in pantry into a kitchen nook.

Zoey is my meticulous secretary and most benevolent critic. We have had a long-running but good-natured dialogue about my failure to sell—"unload" is Zoey's term—the Leland House on Tryon Street. The debate began when I put my foot down and refused to let her order cleanup of the overgrown yard. No prettification, I argued.

"You're the realtor, Dolo," Zoey had insisted. "It's an estate sale. It's your job to market the property. It's not as if Aunt Emmabelle's progeny is going to come out from Buffalo to sweep the floors for you."

She snapped a file drawer shut with the toe of her Naturalizer and tipped her head toward me.

I stepped closer to her and lifted an auburn hair from her Peter Pan collar.

"It doesn't need to be cleaned up, Zoey. That's just the point. Take a good look at it. It's classic Queen Anne—there aren't many left in this valley. It wants an owner who sees through the cosmetic to the potential. I refuse to let it go to somebody who can't do that. I refuse."

I am right about this house, which is breathtaking, even in its disarray. It courts attention with the shabby elegance of a has-been whose coquetry narrowly escapes bad taste. And it is one of a kind, an identical reverse of a second house, which had been constructed on its north side. In 1893, one Judge Johnson Leland built the two homes for his sons, the story went, and demanded that each board foot handled and every inch of wallpaper hung be comparable in the most minute degree so as to alleviate the suspicion of any favoritism. Their partnered position on Tryon Street accounts for what seems to be an imbalance in design in the surviving house.

The curious single tower rising up from the corner gable sheltering the rounded porch on the left makes the entire structure seem like half a house, as though some great hand has smote it down the middle to settle an old score. When I study the house, I see it united with the phantom of its mirror image, razed in the 1930s to make way for a single-story bungalow. If houses were sentient, I've often reflected, the Leland House would be haunted by the absence of its missing mate the way old soldiers are said to sense the ghost of an amputated limb. But when I show the house, if a buyer suggests that symmetry might be better served with the construction of a second tower, I promptly segue the discussion into a forthright exposition of extensive dry rot and antiquated electrical fittings. I do have scruples.

And the house offers one hundred temptations. It has whimsical lathe-turned spindlework rimming the fascia and rounded glass panes in the turret windows and dense plantings of blue iris and black calla lilies and pink naked ladies. So what if the porch planking cants badly to the east? So what if a sheet of graffitied plywood fills in for the missing leaded glass in the front door? So what if the peeling yellow paint falls like spent blossoms into the flower beds? The right buyer, I am certain, will see only the possibilities in the Leland House. The wrong buyer, I am equally certain, is to be quarantined without mercy.

Aunt Emmabelle Leland has left the house in a disheveled state. Zoey's point about progeny is well made: there are none. Aunt Emmabelle departed Woodland for the hereafter without marrying, let alone bearing any more Lelands. The distant cousins in Buffalo take little interest in their California property, and Terry Tanako, the family lawyer in Sacramento, told me, "She's an easy keeper. Take your time."

I am taking my time. Although I didn't let Zoey send over Brian and Hortencia Ochoa, our cleanup crew, I have taken to puttering around the garden, a jungled thicket of overgrown perennials that makes an oasis even in the suffocating valley heat. A grand trumpet vine bearing fluted red cones winds a trunk the size of a man's forearm around the porch balustrade and up the hand-routed pillars. In the oval flower beds to either side of the bricked front walk grow purple and gold columbine and clover-leafed oxalis. I—who can never remember to water a potted pothos before the leaves fall off in utter despair—found myself buying a garden hose and cow manure at Makado's nursery one afternoon in April. And pretty soon I began dropping by in the early evenings to slip my feet into rubber thongs and stand in the steamy shade while I sprinkled the beds, taken in by the flowers with their earnest perseverance, the endurance of their blind trust that someone will care for them. Last week, blood red ranunculus blossoms surprised me, poking through the thready coils of the detritus of several seasons worth of morning glory stalks. As I bent over them to clear the knotted vines, Trevor Tuskes caned his path up the walk.

"Got some anemone rocks here," he said abruptly. "Soak 'em in water overnight, push 'em down about an inch. Make a pretty show. Multiply like crazy. Got to keep 'em wet, though."

Then he caned his way back down the curving bricks, leaving me to open the wrinkled brown lunch bag and shake out the anemone bulbs, dark brown tubers that sat in my hand like misshapen marbles.

So I water the garden and guard the spring colors, but I've left the chipping paint and the broken glass panes. I explain to Zoey that the dilapidation of the Leland House is a test. Whoever passes the test will get the house, it's that simple.

Zoey's repeated rebuttal is that I am not business-minded enough, that I don't seriously respect the profit motive.

"Now, Zoe," I patronized her a few days ago, tapping my fingers on the computer screen where I had just called up two-bedrooms on the east side for Hank Rodriguez's sister.

"Name me a realty in this town that grosses more than we do . . . name me one."

She swiveled her chair around. I kept carping to her back as she punched numbers into her phone.

"Name me one."

Zoey can't. Despite my secret cattiness and unconscionable elitism on matters of taste, I can sell houses. Whether it's a two-thousand-dollar-down starter home in Sunwest Subdivision (take your pick of hi-lo carpet: blue, green, or gold) or a four-thousand-square-foot ranch style with semidetached in-law quarters and RV parking, I can find buyers. Not just any buyers, but those who will, years later, recall with fondness the absolute conviction with which I led them to the house that won their hearts. I work with a poet's grasp of the concrete and an instinct for deciphering details. I can foresee, for instance, that a husband and wife who wear his and her white Nikes will invariably take the remodel with the wet bar . . . such equations seem to me evidence of a cosmic scheme in which every human being has a perfect counterpart. The descriptive language with which I depict a fixer-upper for a well-heeled client is different from that I use to entice a handyman. Husbands who seek three-car garages inevitably want low-care garden systems. (Do I happen to know the name of the previous owners' gardener, by the way?) Even though I earn Zoey's pious reprimands for my chronically unkind characterizations, I know what people want. Or if not that, what they ought to want.

The Walters don't want the Leland House, of this I am sure.

"Why don't we look into the cellar," I suggest to Phil Walters, who is banging away at the rusty trap under the kitchen sink. I long to ask him whether kicking tires works, too, but I think of Zoey and smile sweetly instead.

"I think you'll want to get a sense of just how much repair is necessary, Phil. Sometimes these old houses need to be rebuilt from the ground up."

Tammy Walters takes her husband's hand.

"That's just what we wanted, isn't it, babe?"

She turns to me.

"Phil and I were saying on the way up here that we want something we could do up all modern . . . my brother-in-law is a carpenter? And him and Phil could work on weekends . . . it'd be like camping, wouldn't it, honey?"

"You'd live here while you remodeled?" I make the words slow, incredulous. I sigh and draw open the front door, which drags as it fans across the parquet entry. I bend down to scrape a fingernail against the oak flooring.

"These old floors take so much work . . ." apologetic now, woman to woman to Tammy.

"You're always buffing or dusting or shellacking or something . . . but it's worth it to have an old house, isn't it?"

Tammy frowns.

"Maybe we could just do wall-to-wall."

Phil stomps a one-two-three rhythm on the porch planking.

"Oh, watch that, Phil."

I take his arm.

"Don't want you falling through—the joists down there are pretty shaky."

I tell Phil that city codes will prohibit them from blacktopping the front yard so Phil can park his four-wheel-drive stepside next to Tammy's Suburban. And that two roof trusses on the eastern eave appear to be cracking. I don't need to bring up the sewer lines. By the time we reach the sidewalk, Phil and Tammy Walters have lost most of their enthusiasm for Victorian architecture.

The basement tour isn't necessary, but I do, after all, intend to make a sale.

"I have a house in the Brookside development that I think you'll like. It has an interesting raised platform in the master bedroom."

I lead the way to the company Buick and unlock the passenger door for Tammy.

"Can you send some air back here?" Phil asks from the backseat as I pull the sedan away from the curb.

"Sure." I raise my window and punch open the rear vent.

"You know, Phil, getting central air into these old two-stories is next to impossible. You're wise to look at something newer. . . . Shall we try next Saturday? Some of the older Brookside homes do have kitchen nooks."

Tammy reaches into the backseat to squeeze Phil's hand. "Whatever the wife wants is fine with me."

"Saturday's on, then."

I sit in the Buick and watch the Walters pull away from the office in their black Suburban. I make myself a mental note to run the Brookside listings in the two hundred range before next Saturday. For some people, I consider without envy, money may help to buy a sort of happiness. For me, it seems to have bought only a lackluster seven-year affair with insurance mogul Henry Talmouth, an affair I am ending effective today.

I pull the Buick into the company garage and step into the sun. Lifting a hand to signal to Zoey that I am done for the day, I face my reflection in the plate glass window that fronts the realty. My curly hair has tumbled from its clip. The loose plaid sundress I chose carelessly this morning seems to be losing half its hem, giving me an off-kilter look that is surely driving Zoey crazy. If I take off my prescription sunglasses, I think I can squint myself back into my twenties, to the Dolores Meredith I was before Henry Talmouth, before the inexorably dawning realization that I have never, in all my life, met a man whom I could call "babe," who would call me in return "the wife." What does Henry Talmouth see in me? I ask myself. Is it my six-figure income that salves his conscience when he cancels out on me for the sake of the wife and kids? Is it my ability to forget him for days on end so that he never has to fear the badly timed phone call invading his other private life? Is it simply that my expectations of him are, damn it all, nearly nonexistent?

My thoughts take a morbid turn as I walk across the street to the walnut tree under which I have parked my old Volvo, a 77— my first car—bought after graduate school and my second year of earning top commissions with Parker, Aubrey, and Downes. I hadn't intended to become a money-grubbing yuppie. Somehow the years after my thesis project have stacked themselves one upon the other until here I am, clinging to an artifact that reminds me in another age I had hoped for different things.

I had hoped, for starters, to have a husband and a family by now, before the ticking of the biological clock pushed me irrevocably into a status I share unwillingly but resignedly with Aunt Emmabelle. I had hoped that the early promise of my undergraduate writing courses would entitle me to a literary life, but it hadn't. I wince afresh when I recall the afternoon that Dr. Chalmers, my project adviser, called me into his office at Cal and pronounced judgment—I hung on his every word—on my poems. He held my manuscript, painstakingly typed on the old Smith Corona with which Daddy had sent me off to college after christening it with his faith: the West Coast twentieth-century Emily Dickinson, he'd called me. Dr. Chalmers had trouble relighting his pipe. I stared at his hands, their thick fingers and the wiry black hair that seemed more suited to a carpenter than an academic.

"These are admirable poems, Dolores. Good solid work. You deserve an A for the project, and that's what I'm recommending."

He didn't have to say more. I knew if there had been more to say, I would have heard it. He was a scholar and a gentle man, and he tried to temper my disappointment by encouraging me to go into teaching. I'd be good in the classroom, he predicted. I was a good reader and a good critic, he offered. When I considered defying his boding, when I envisioned the bleak prospect of living hand-to-mouth with the company of my Smith-Corona and the rejection slips which were bound to come, I retreated. Not to a classroom— that would have been too depressing—but to take stock of my talents. Nearly twenty years later, I have parlayed myself into a dealer of metaphor and symbolism, of hyperbole and oxymoron. I have done very well, and I have learned to hope for less and less.

I hadn't hoped for Henry Talmouth, but I got him. I open the Volvo's doors to let whatever stray wind there might be clear the compressed heat. The air conditioner went down, and, stubborn, I let it go, just as I had let go the sunroof, the passenger-side door handle, and the odometer. I like the stripped feeling of downsizing, the lightness I feel when people exclaim, "But you're a realtor! And you live in a rented apartment!" In some way my diction can't articulate, my eccentricities keep me faithful to myself and the poet I once wanted to be.

Shedding Henry Talmouth is giving me the same lightness, a floating feeling that takes me to Smokes and Spirits to buy a bottle of good Chianti and then leads me back to the Leland House, where I take the front door key from the lockbox and let myself in. The parlor catches the light of the lowering sun. It shines through the elm trees lining Tryon Street and dapples the mantled fireplace with waltzing patterns of light and dark. The house is warm with the heated musk of a century; I think the still air is suffocating in a comfortable sort of way, the same way I derived comfort when, as a small child, I would pull up the hood of my sleeping bag and breathe in the warm mist of my own exhaled breath.

I rummage through my bag and find my Swiss Army knife. My older brother, Todd, gave it to me the day after Daddy's funeral. Two of the blades have been snapped off by Todd in his teenage years, put to some illegal use, undoubtedly, but the corkscrew remains trustworthy.

We held the wake in the old Sacramento house, the rambling two-story in which Todd and I were raised, motherless but well loved. We flew home together from our colleges on the East Coast to bury our father. The only specific memory I hold of the two weeks during which Todd and I settled the estate was the day Todd found me sorting my mother's china.

"I don't want any of this stuff," I said to him, awash in a small sea of crumpled newspapers and stacked teacups. "I feel guilty, but I don't want it." I traced the gold filigree lining the rim of a fragile bowl that we had never, in all my childhood, allowed to be tainted by the touch of foodstuff.

"Give it away, Do. It doesn't matter. He wouldn't mind." He had held me then, my big brother, and put the knife, wet with tears, into my hand.

"Remember the summers in Donner? Remember how he let us

take whatever we wanted to eat, as long as it was in a can?" Todd rocked me against him.

"Vienna sausages and Spaghetti Os," I answered him.

"Good old Vienna sausages," echoed Todd. "Keep the knife instead of the china."

I kept it, and with it the touchstone of my father, a man who could heft his five-year-old daughter onto his shoulders and hike four miles without cease in the high Sierra. A man whose bedtime tales leaned to booming recitations from *Paradise Lost*. A man whose only requirements of his children were that they live happy and leave the world a better place. A man against whom I measure all other men and whom, I am afraid, I have failed in some way he would never acknowledge.

"Oh, Daddy." I sit down cross-legged in the dust of the marred oak floor. "You have so spoiled me."

I twist and turn the corkscrew and pull the cork piece by piece from the Chianti. Before I sip from the used Dixie cup I found in the Volvo's trunk, I float the cork chips from the surface.

"I may not be able to open a bottle of wine," I toast the air, "but I sure know how to sell a house."

Then I know I am going to cry.

Henry Talmouth isn't a bad man. He hasn't used me in any way that I haven't let myself be used. He can be courtly, he can be funny, he drives very nice cars — but he isn't the one. I used to hope that he would be. Early on, I deluded myself into thinking that perhaps he was, but when the affair settled into habit and even the illicit tête-à-têtes grew predictable, the sad truth was unavoidable.

I am not and have never been in love with Henry Talmouth. Henry Talmouth doesn't read anything except *Kiplinger*. Henry Talmouth prefers steel and glass furniture to mahogany. Henry Talmouth thinks I should bob my unruly hair. Henry Talmouth does not make me happy. For the last two years I have settled for convenience. Now solitude seems preferable.

I pour a second cup of the wine and lie back against the warm oak flooring. The tears roll down my cheeks. They must be making tiny dusty drops on the floor of my most hallowed listing. The Leland House is utterly still except for the dancing pattern of sunlight on the fireplace wall. I cross my hands on my chest and shut my eyes.

I have made for myself a bad match.

CHAPTER TWO

My life had stood——a loaded gun

~

My Life had stood—a Loaded Gun—
In Corners—till a Day
The Owner passed—identified—
And carried Me away—

And now We roam in Sovereign Woods—
And now We hunt the Doe—
And every time I speak for Him—
The Mountains straight reply—

And do I smile, such cordial light
Upon the Valley glow—
It is as a Vesuvian face
Had let its pleasure through—

And when at Night—Our good Day done—
I guard My Master's Head—
Tis better than the Eider-Duck's
Deep Pillow—to have shared—

To foe of His—I'm deadly foe—
None stir the second time—
On whom I lay a Yellow Eye—
Or an emphatic Thumb—

Though I than He—may longer live
He longer must—than I—
For I have but the power to kill,
Without—the power to die—

EMILY DICKINSON 1863

IT WILL NOT be hard for me to leave New York City.

Tucked into the mirror frame of the worn oak dresser in my Manhattan apartment, I keep a dog-eared photograph of a tall, darkly bearded kid. He is perched on a gray rock next to a stand of enormous pines. He shoulders a bulging forest green backpack, from which hang a blue-tinned cup, the broken-down rods of a fishing pole, and a plastic bag sagging with the weight of a hardbound book. Behind the boy, a rocky Sierran ledge is profiled in the glass oval of an alpine lake. The shooter has made a good joke. The tanned boy smiles into the camera, as if he is entering the most beautiful country in the world.

I am that boy. The photograph was taken by my father the autumn I left Woodland for Dartmouth, two weeks before he died quickly, professionally, at his desk in the Sutter Laboratories, divining his own fate in the murky agar of his petri dishes, his head bending lower and lower. We had come through Donner Pass to Emigrant Gap after eight days of backpacking. The world lay before me, I told my father, "like a land of dreams." Two weeks after the sunlight glanced through the aperture and fixed forever my hopeful image on film—even before my mother had time to reclaim the developed photographs at Woodland Drugs—my father, Daniel Barclay, was dead.

The photo went with me to Dartmouth, where I used it to erase the unreasonable final knowledge I took from my father's premature death, Matthew Arnold's prophecy made mortal flesh. It went with me to Yale Law, where I graduated sixth in my class and came to believe that the legal word proffered unshifting sands in an otherwise deceitful universe. It went with me to the two-room apartment in Greenwich Village where I lived during the three years that I clerked for Federal Judge Amos Thomas Jefferson, and again with me when I moved uptown and made youngest partner in history at Vickers and Mallory, Corporate Law, Inc. At once a talisman and a stigma, the photograph of the grinning boy on the cusp of manhood is drawing me west, drawing me home. At forty-one, I have resolved that I am finally wealthy and lonely enough to give up New York to return to California.

"Mister Austin, the telephone is for you."

Lupe pushes open the bedroom door, sliding with it a half-filled box of tousled sweaters.

"You cannot pack this things these way," she scolds me. "Take the phone in the kitchen and I will do it."

I stand up from the cedar chest, where I have been sitting as I toss balled-up sweaters and T-shirts into the gaping boxes cluttering the floor of my bedroom. Lupe is right—I'm not much of a packer.

"Ah, Lupe . . . what will you do when you don't have me to boss around anymore?"

I hug her to me, this tiny woman who has been my housekeeper and spiritual counsel for over a decade. She cures self-pity with *mole de guajolote*, admonishes my slovenly habits with Spanish language abandon, and just once, during Mom's doomed siege with ovarian cancer, held me against her and whispered *mijo, mijo, mijo*. Lupe I will miss as much as anyone in New York, but she refuses to consider coming west with me.

"Retire, that's what I do. The phone, Mister Austin!"

"Okay, I'm out of here—" In a backward overhead pitch, I lob one last sweatshirt into the box behind me.

"From Meadowlark Lemon to you, Lupe!"

She picks up a wrinkled dress shirt. For a moment I think she will pass it to me in play, but she waves me from the bedroom.

I pick up the phone in Lupe's immaculate white kitchen, where tall aluminum windows open to a panorama of the treetops of Central Park. No comparison to the view of Lake Spaulding from the peak of Brady Mountain, I think with a rush of anticipation. And I won't miss the dishonest film of city street soot, or the bellicose cabbies, or the incessant hum of automation everywhere I turn, inside and out. I wonder how I have lived as long as I have in this archetypal city when the blood of California farmers courses through my veins.

"Austin." Jack Mariani's heartiest boardroom bellow issues through the wire. "I played racquetball with a couple of fellows from City's law school this afternoon . . . they tell me there's a very happy dean out in the Sacramento Valley . . ."

"They've got themselves one happy hire out here."

"And you leave next week, no second thoughts?"

"No second thoughts, sir." I slide Lupe's Cuisinart along the white counter tiles with my free hand, then slide it back and re-turn to the view of the park.

"Of course I'm not eager to leave the firm . . . but if you're look-ing for early regrets, I can't confess to any, no, Jack."

"Son, then you couldn't be in a better position. As much as we value you—well, you've heard me through this eulogy before. I'm not calling to badger you—Clair wanted me to be sure you knew the dinner is on for the twenty-seventh."

"I have it on my calendar—seven?"

"Seven it is. Clair says we'll pick you up. And Austin?"

"Jack?"

"You have our blessing, you know that."

Jack Mariani is in the habit of giving me his blessing. Seven years ago, during the Randco-Temtech merger, upon Jack's insis-tence and bolstered by his unwavering fatherly faith in my capa-bilities, I assumed the position of senior attorney when Delbert Mallory suffered a massive heart attack three days before the oral argument to the court of appeals. The corporation's argument tri-umphed, Jack unclenched his nervously balled fists, and I went on to handle more of the firm's most troublesome litigation. Last year, again with Jack's urging, I rewrote an advocacy brief to incorpo-rate an analysis of the court's opinion. The *Harvard Law Review* picked up the article, the dean at the UC Davis Law School saw my work and made an offer, and now I am exiting corporate prac-tice to return to the classroom as faculty. In a circular irony that Jack was the first to recognize, he set into motion the means by which I am returning to California and leaving Vickers and Mallory. That he has been absolutely gracious throughout is ample blessing, and I have told him as much.

I lean my forehead against the cool glass of the kitchen pane. My choice has fallen into place, the coalescence of the offer to teach law and the stirrings of some long-buried desire to engage in the more human give-and-take of the law school classroom. The balance tipped when I considered the contrast between the texture of daily life on the Upper East Side and in a town like Woodland. Once granted the opportunity to imagine the fit of life in California, I let myself yearn for what my memory seemed to have forgotten but my senses had not: the peppery smell of first-cut alfalfa in the valley, the satisfying crunch of shale under a boot, the company of townfolk who had stayed put for generations and could trace my genealogy as accurately as their own.

I can't remember when I last spent a weekend hiking . . . I don't know whether I own a backpack anymore. Even though I have been jogging for years, my skin preserves a Wall Street pallor because the only hour my day allows me running time is at five in the morning, when a team of silent hackers and I take to the paths of Central Park. There is no allowance in the corporate agenda for mountain weekends. Of late, I have begun to dwell on memories of my father, of the muscular physique that would garner approval from even the most rigorous contemporary health police. Time outran him, I grew to comprehend, simply because the laboratory robbed so many vital hours from the real business of living. I will miss Jack, but the choice is right.

In April when I flew back to California for interviews with the law school faculty, I rented a Toyota at the Sacramento Airport and headed up Interstate 5 to the town in which I was raised. Woodland's periphery is extended by garish, sprawling strip malls, many of them powered, no doubt, by the companies for which I have litigated. But the town's heart, tidier than I remembered, has been restored with historical reverence. I parked the Toyota on Avery Street, across from Caitlin Lamb's house, in the reenactment of a habit I performed throughout my senior year of high school as I waited for my girl, the prettiest in Woodland High and the sole serious love of my life.

We were sitting in that very spot when Caitlin turned to me, brushed her blonde bangs from her eyes, and told me solemnly that when I left for Dartmouth she was going to work at Hansen's Pipe and Well Drilling and would probably be married to Kenny Hansen by the time I returned. She soothsaid accurately, except that after my father's death and my mother's remarriage I really never did return, not for nearly twenty years. Caitlin somehow catalyzed the very chemical of character that she recognized and feared in me—the serious, steadfast application to task which warned a woman away but made me into the whiz kid of corporate law. Back in April I wondered then, as I do now, if Caitlin's making a different choice would have altered my course, whether we'd be together still or bitterly disengaged. I wonder too whether I might be returning to Woodland for a second chance, for the opportunity to seize again the expectation I abandoned when Caitlin turned to me and laid her soft hand on my knee.

Lupe startles me from reverie with a touch to my shoulder.

"Turkey sandwich? Cobb salad? Quiche?"

"Salad's fine." I turn from the window.

"Can you find the tux for me, Lupe? The dinner is next week—"

"Hanging on the closet door. In the bag." Lupe bats me away from the refrigerator door.

Even as she shoos me from the kitchen, I can see her standing on the couch to reach my bowtie, which she will align perfectly with the white boutonniere she will remember to order from Fiamma's Florals. Lupe I will miss.

Clair Mariani has reserved the Bagatelle for my farewell dinner. In her perceptive but mannered way, she arranges the evening so that she and Jack will pick me up. To her, I have long ago deciphered, I am an incorrigible unmatchable bachelor—silent at the wrong moment, garrulous when a conversation demands pause, completely graceless in the pursuit of romance. By arriving with the guest of honor, soon to be resident of the Wild West, Clair has relieved herself of the duty of finding one final suitable escort for me, a man who, she once hissed to Jack over crème brûlée for four, doesn't have one iota of an idea about the rules of courtship.

"Maybe he's not interested in this one," Jack had defended me.

"Maybe he's a legal orator without the barest inkling of how to speak to women," Clair had retorted. "Can't you teach him anything, Jack?"

After several weeks of racquetball and the sweaty exchanges of the sauna room, Jack reported to Clair what he'd always reckoned but had now verified: that I pined in some illogical, adolescent way for the high school girl who'd chosen another—and for the wholehearted certainty of the kind of feeling that a teenager musters so readily but a grown man learns to distrust. For the sake of literary resolution and Clair's mollification, Jack added a tragic touch: never having met a woman who evoked from me the earnest devotion I felt toward Caitlin Lamb, I remained single. End of investigation.

Clair would be surprised to hear that I have done some marital analysis of my own, that I am not the complete bumpkin she would have me be. For years, I have studied her with Jack, their barbed exchanges which land like heat-seeking missiles drawn to targets confirmed by forty years of covert reconnaisance. I love Jack because he has been both a brother and a father to me, but neither he nor Clair is aptly cast as a player in the model marriage. I have seen their guerrilla wars last for months; I have seen Jack so worn from the daily skirmishes that I have been tempted to tell him to pack a bag and move in with me—to argue my case that solitude must indeed be preferable to the relationship he has with Clair. But convenience can masquerade as devotion, and I have held my tongue out of respect for whatever it is that Jack Mariani needs.

Clair tsked at Jack's rendition of my romantic condition, raised an eyebrow, and effected one last arrangement, a pair of theater tickets Jack shunted off on me with the name and phone number of a family friend: Julie Tyndel, blonde, twenty-nine, twelfth in her class at Cal's Boalt Hall. After the exchange, she swore to Jack she had washed her hands of the chore of marrying off Austin Barclay.

Convenience, I confess to myself, can also masquerade as companionship, as desire. I took Julie to the theater, and then to dinners, and then to movie openings. In the dead of winter, we went on a weekend upstate when the snow didn't stop falling for thirty-six hours. Bundle up and come on out, I coaxed her, but she didn't like the snow. When I discovered that she didn't really like being outside in fair weather or foul, when we ran out of things to talk about, I stopped calling. I am not proud to say that I didn't return her calls, either, but it was how I handled it. I may not be suave enough for Clair, but I'm not cruel. I wasn't about to tell Julie that I just didn't feel anything for her, that I tried but couldn't. Indifference seems to me a greater slight that dislike.

The evening at Bagatelle's is easier, since Clair has given up on me, since I've rendered myself a nonissue. She and Jack are charming hosts when they set aside the vendetta. My spirit lightens as the move to California grows sharper and the duties of the law firm fade.

I rise from my seat to the civilized demands for speech! speech! which dwindle to respectful silence after Jack taps a spoon against his empty wineglass. As I survey the lavish restaurant and the faces of colleagues and clients, as a fork clatters onto china and the rustle of linen napkins stills, I realize that for all the familiarity embracing me, I know these people very little. I have never told Jack, the closest friend of my adult life, of the spiral notebooks filled with blank verse composed during my first two years in Greenwich Village. With none of these men have I shared a canteen of warm water after a day of hiking, easy without words in the absence of shrilling telephones and the buzz of fax machines. I have argued, lobbied, negotiated, compromised—but rarely befriended any of the polite people who wait on my delivery.

On the plane to San Francisco, I can't recall much of what I said, except that Andrew Marvell's lines from "The Garden" came to me as a closing device:

> *How vainly men themselves amaze*
> *To win the palm, the oak, or bays,*
> *And their incessant labors see*
> *Crowned from some single herb, or tree,*
> *Whose short and narrow-verged shade*
> *Does prudently their toils upbraid—*

A good attorney, considering my audience, I cut short before "garlands of repose"—the line doesn't work when there is life yet to be lived. Literary accuracy doesn't matter here anyway—poetry being of little consequence in the corporate landscape. How quickly I find myself turning Californian, I think, as the applause rises and falls.

Coffee is served from silver service. I stand and sit and stand again to receive the initial farewell handshake. When I turn from Sawyer Martin to take Elise McDonald's jeweled hand, I see Julie Tyndel rise from her chair at a small table in the back of the room. Clair's opinions of my social graces are harsh, but she has never been able to fault me for rudeness. When I see Julie rise and head so obviously toward the cloakroom, I break my handshake with Mark Epstein, clap him on the back, and excuse myself.

"Julie?" I dodge welcoming faces and take her arm as she turns to me.

"Hello again, Austin," she says without meeting my eyes.

"I'd like to say good-bye . . . to apologize . . ."

"No need."

"It didn't work," I offer lamely.

"I guessed as much when you didn't return my calls."

This time Julie looks up at me so that even in the subdued lighting of the Bagatelle I can see the half-circles of shadow under her eyes.

"Have you been . . . okay?" I let go of her arm as she walks to the lobby.

"Well, you know Bookman's . . . they work first-year lawyers like hell."

Julie hands her ticket to the clerk, waits for her wrap.

"I'm sorry. Not about the work—about the other. You're a—it was my—"

"No need, Austin," she repeats to interrupt me. "Don't say anything, please. I'm leaving. I'm tired."

I hold her coat as she shrugs into it.

"Good luck, Austin. Happy life."

I watch her through the whirling door, then turn back to the crowd and catch Clair Mariani's hawklike eye.

One week later, in the westbound plane lifting from La Guardia, I think again of Julie's pretty, exhausted face. Myself ten years ago, I solace the surge of guilt, and vow that the first thing I will do upon arrival in California is to order a top-of-the-line backpack from REI and call a realtor to find a house.

Not in Davis, not Sacramento—Woodland. Something old, something classic, something I can work at renovating in the two months before fall semester. In a real neighborhood, where fathers rake leaves and the kites of little boys hang up in the limbs of a neighbor's trees. Where the street is calm and the screen door is left open for the dog. Maybe a Victorian. With oak floors and an overgrown yard.

A home.

CHAPTER THREE

One and one——are one——

☙

One and One—are One—
Two—be finished using—
Well enough for Schools—
But for Minor Choosing—

Life—just—Or Death—
Or the Everlasting—
More—would be too vast
For the Soul's Comprising—

EMILY DICKINSON 1863

THE FLUTTERING AGAINST my heart raises me from sleep. For a moment before I open my eyes, the faintest arrhythmia of pinpricks upon my skin warns me of something I have forgotten, some undone task sinking deep into the dark soul of my subconscious. I awake to Milton, whose gray paws are making bread against my chest. His face tilts toward me, and I lift my hand to stroke his fur, backbrushing the diamond-shaped patch of white hair that covers the scar on his left side. Milton is silent, a cat who makes his desires felt with the irritated switch of a tail or the deliberate placement of a heavy paw. He was silent two years ago, when I picked him up from the corner of a deserted garage on the east side where, I am sure, he had laid himself down to die. He'd had a cruel gash running from his back to his belly—the swipe of a shovel?—so festering that he must have given up on trying to clean himself and instead dragged his tabby hide into a dark nest of oily rags to die in peace. His dignity amazed me throughout the trip to the vet's and the long recuperation from eighteen internal stitches and twenty-four external ones. He'd clearly lived a full life, the vet said then, did I really want to spend the money to fix him up? I did. Milton's still here, where he wears his diamond patch with the same mute dignity and wakes me every morning with the motor of his purring and his paws against my skin.

I disengage his claws from my T-shirt and sit up, hefting his warm weight against my chest. I know his limits—I know how long I can cuddle him before the tail switch signals that he's had enough babying, but I take what I can—his prorated payments for love tendered long ago—and head for the kitchen.

"Okay, Milton. Tuna or kidney?"

When the can opener whines open the kidney, Milton stands against my bare leg, claws sheathed, to stress his impatience. The phone rings as I bend to shake out yesterday's unread *Daily Democrat* and position his bowl on a front-page photograph of George Bush's face, my concession to tidiness. The phone rings again, and I remember what today is: the first day of my life after Henry Talmouth. I let the machine answer.

"Dolores? I know you're there. And you're being absolutely unreasonable. Let me pick you up for lunch—between two and four—I'm not sure when I'll be back from Vacaville—give me a call, Dolores."

Now that I have officially declared myself independent from Henry Talmouth, I can afford to criticize his style. Between two and four is quite a window, Hen. Taking a bit much for granted, don't you think? But I resist picking up the phone to tell him so.

Milton is licking his bowl clean. The anemone bulbs that Trevor Tuskes gave me are soaking in a mug of water. I pour the water through the drain of my fingers and feel the bulbs. They have softened up, so I set up six peat pots filled with a mixment of steer manure and potting soil on the windowsill and push the bulbs in to the depth Trevor instructed me. The phone rings again. I slowly rinse the soil from my fingers under warm water. It is Henry, phone call number two.

"Dolores, it can't be lunch. This is ridiculous! Pick up the phone so I can talk with you! The kids have a softball game, and I don't want to miss the first pitch—damn you, Dolores! Pick up the phone so we can discuss this!"

I let Milton out the kitchen door and watch him tightrope the mowing strip that curbs the tiny back lawn of the apartment. He is graceful for such a heavy cat, and when he sits to lick an extended rear leg, I decide to join him in the sun. I put water for coffee on the stove and slip through the door. The phone rings a third time. He's persistent, I'll grant him that. Hates losing, is what it is. The losing, not the loss, bothers Henry Talmouth.

Henry's voice booms through the screen door.

"Dolores. This is the last time I'm calling. You're behaving childishly. I mean this, Dolores, I will not call again. If you want to speak with me, you'll have to call me yourself."

Oh, Henry. Milton has more self-respect than you.

When the teakettle whistles, I return to the kitchen and filter the hot water through the coffee grinds. The phone rings a fourth time, but I take my cup to the bedroom and study the open door of my closet. What to wear, what to wear. I don't have a closing, I don't have a showing . . . it doesn't really matter what I wear today. Zoey will criticize my incapacity to dress like an adult, but I pull out an embroidered Mexican blouse and a pair of jeans. The phone stops ringing and the machine picks up. I move into the bathroom and turn on the shower.

"Dolores? This is Arinda Mesa. We have seven children signed up for the poetry workshop. I need to reserve the community room. Could you call the center to schedule? I'll be in until—"

I skid into the kitchen and snag the phone.

"Hello, Arinda, I'm here—"

"Good morning, Dolores. We have seven second-graders signed up for the children's poetry workshop—did anyone let you know?"

"Not until now. That's wonderful. Do think we'll get more?"

Arinda explains to me the logistics. I have offered to teach a poetry workshop for migrant children in the Hispanic Community Center downtown. What prompted me to volunteer isn't clear to me even now, but when Zoey mentioned that she was doing bilingual tutoring in math, the idea started to take shape. Arinda Mesa says that the class may have as many as twelve children, but I have to be prepared to see them come and go without regularity. And that some of the parents will use the class as a baby-sitting agency. I haven't told Arinda the reservations I have about myself, the ex-lit major who refused to consider spending her talents in the classroom. We'll be even, I guess, the children and I. We set the class for two hours on Wednesday afternoons. I'll be happy to bring snacks, I tell her.

When I hang up the phone, Milton is standing against the screen door, my signal that I ought to be leaving for work. I let him in, rinse and refill his water bowl, and return to the shower. When I have dressed and run a comb through my damp hair, I see that he has settled down into the crumpled sheets of my unmade bed. He'll sleep there until I come home, when we'll repeat the feeding ritual. As I leave the apartment, the phone rings again. Milton will have to deal with Henry today. I refuse.

Zoey does give me the once-over when I arrive at the office, but instead of criticizing my attire she hands me two bank statements, a letter from the county recorder, and a cup of milky coffee. Zoey is weaning me from my caffeine, and she thinks that if she cleverly dilutes the coffee with more and more milk, I will eventually stop craving the caffeine. I look down at the milky potion and up to meet Zoey's eyes.

"Dolores. You need the calcium, not the caffeine."

"Thanks a bunch, Zoey. My dowager's hump that bad today?" I pull my calendar toward me to note the Wednesday afternoon poetry class. "Arinda Mesa called this morning. She says there are seven children signed up for the workshop."

Zoey raises an eyebrow. "You're really going to teach the class, then?"

"It looks like it. I think we'll be evenly matched for dedication.

She says that they may not attend regularly . . . that the parents may be using the course as day care . . ."

"Then you do what you can with what you have," Zoey piously reminds me. "This isn't about you, Dolores. It's about the children."

"I know, I know. I do *know* that, Zoey. I'm just unsure of what skills I can muster at this late date. They'll hardly be wanting to do psychobiography of Sylvia Plath, which is what we covered in the last course I recall taking."

Zoey rolls her eyes. "They are children, Dolores. Remember that. Children for whom school has not necessarily been a very pleasant experience. Don't forget that they want to learn if you make it rewarding to them."

Zoey means well, and she's absolutely right, but I know that this kind of abstraction is what steered me away from pedagogy. Instead of learning outcomes, I think of Emily Dickinson in her garden and Plath's instructions to birth a poem in the immediate specific details of daily life. For the first session, I'm planning to bring in a tray of elements from the garden at the Leland House: buds and blossoms, twigs and leaves, rocks and soil, leftover seed pods. We'll write a growing poem. I cross my fingers and hope my lesson makes pedagogical sense.

I am studying the bank statements when the phone rings. Zoey picks up.

"Good morning. Meredith Realty . . . yes. Yes, we do. The broker is here. Just a moment please." Zoey raises her head. I punch open my line.

"Good morning. This is Dolores Meredith. What can I help you with?"

"My name is Austin Barclay. I'm looking for an older house in downtown Woodland. Do you have anything like that?"

"I think we do. Tell me a little more about what you want."

"I want something that could use work . . . a big yard . . . wooden floors. Lots of light."

"Size?"

"I'm single. Size isn't such an issue. I'll need an office, so a couple of bedrooms would be good. What I'm really after is . . . character. And two stories. Does this suggest anything like what you may be listing?"

I repeat, "Needs work, big yard, wooden floors, two stories . . . I think we may have something that will please you. Are you new to Woodland?"

His voice is easy, straightforward. "I guess you'd say new . . . maybe returning is a better description. I'm moving back from the East. I used to know Woodland well, when I was a kid."

"Price range?"

"Nothing ostentatious—money's not the object. What I really want is something . . . something I can bring back from the dead."

"You remember Tryon Street? Big elms, sidewalks, picket fences?"

"Sure."

"Why don't we schedule an appointment, and I'll show you what we have in town."

We talk for a moment longer. He is a law professor, starting at Davis in the fall. I make an appointment for tomorrow. Austin Barclay/Leland? I write on my calendar, 10:00.

I hang up the phone and swivel toward Zoey. "This may be the one, Zoe. He's looking for downtown . . . in need of repair. I'm going to show him the Leland House tomorrow. This may be the one!"

Zoey bites her tongue for a minute, then lets loose.

"I told you you should have fixed that front porch, cleaned that trash out of the back shed—"

"No, no, no, Zoey. He wants shabby! Just wait—I think he'll pass the test! I think I've found the buyer!"

"Tests," she says, disbelieving. "I hope you get over your test fixation before your workshop. For a free spirit, Dolores, you are amazingly rule bound. Tests."

I am thinking of tests the following morning when I face my closet again. First impressions are tests, too, so I am relatively careful with my clothes when I introduce myself to a client. I pull a silk blouse from the hanger. It needs ironing, but it will do. A dark skirt.

Hose and heels. I have just straightened out the cover on my bed so that I can assess the reputability of my outfit when a series of soft thuds resounds from the kitchen.

Milton is sitting on the kitchen counter next to the can opener, his tail twitching, his eyes angry slits. The peat pots holding Trevor Tuske's anemone bulbs are overturned on the linoleum, whipped there by Milton, whom I have forgotten to feed.

"Sorry, Milts, sorry." I grab a can of cat food, open it, and sling it into Milton's bowl. Then, because I don't have an extra second and it is my nature to dwell in small disasters, I slice my finger neatly on the razor-sharp lid. In the seconds before the flawless incision begins to bleed, I wrap my finger with a paper towel, haul my sullen Milton back from the edge of the counter, and slide the bowl under his chin.

"Eat this here, Milton. Please."

There is potting soil coating the floor, and if I don't get it up it will be all over the apartment as soon as Milton pads through it. Again, I am cursed to be running late, but I rinse and tape my finger with the only Band-Aids in my medicine cabinet— Disney cartoons—and take the time to sweep up the dirt, reset the bulbs in their pots, and sponge the linoleum. No time for coffee, barely time to shower. I press the blouse as best I can and run out to the Volvo. I may make my ten o'clock appointment with Austin Barclay, just barely. This is a test I don't want to fail.

I clip the speed limit across town and wheel into the Volvo's parking place under the walnut tree. I start across the street to the realty's garage, then remember that I have forgotten the Buick keys, which I keep in the glove box of the Volvo. Back to the Volvo, I retrieve the keys and sprint to the garage. I start the Buick, back it from the garage, and position it neatly in front of the realty's front window. I run back to shut the garage door, shoulder my bag, and tear into the office.

Zoey is standing by the door, holding the Leland House file.

"My blouse, please, Zoey. Do up my blouse."

Zoey heaves a sigh of futility and buttons the little pearl closures up my back. When she is done, she sighs again and turns me around.

"Mr. Barclay, this is Dolores Meredith."

He is standing in the shadow of Zoey's enormous ficus tree, so I didn't realize he was there at all. He has been viewing me from the window, watching my helter-skelter approach, every embarrassing, unprofessional, tardy inch of it.

"Pleased to meet you" is all I can manage as I extend my hand and step across the office. "Sorry I'm late—"

"No, I was early. I wasn't sure how long it would take for me to get my bearings, so I was early. Don't worry."

He is smiling. I realize that I have been holding his hand far too long, but before I drop it, I look down and think to myself that this hand I am clasping is Dr. Chalmers's—broad and strong, dark haired, the hand of a carpenter.

"Well, it is nice to meet you. Welcome to California. Or welcome back to California. I have a beautiful house for you—I think I mentioned Tryon Street to you?"

He is still smiling, and I realize that Zoey is staring at me because I am gushing. I am breaking my cardinal rule of sales—I am setting up an expectation before I really know the buyer. Ordinarily I sit down behind my desk, Zoey brings coffee, and we chat about the town, about family, about schools and taxes if necessary—but I never set my buyers up. Zoey reads my mind and steps forward with damage control.

"I'll get coffee? Do you take yours black, Mr. Barclay?"

"Just milk, thanks."

"Dolores?"

"Just milk, thanks." Repeating his order, I feel an absolute dolt. I prefer my coffee black, and my self-appointed osteological guardian knows it. I am flustering myself. Behind Austin Barclay's back, Zoey is gagging herself with a finger, then slashing her throat. Straighten up, the grisly sign language says. Get with the program.

"Have a seat." I gesture to the padded chair in front of my desk. I shrug out of my bag. Austin Barclay lowers himself comfortably into the chair. He doesn't look like a professor; he looks like a mountaineer, a cowboy, a logger. He is wearing worn jeans and a Bruce Springsteen T-shirt. His forehead and arms look faintly sunburned. His dark curly hair is too long to please the law school, I expect, and it seems that he hasn't shaved this morning. This man is not the bespectacled, timid, gray-haired scholar I expected. I damn the badly ironed silk blouse I am wearing and the Mickey Mouse caricature on my finger that Austin Barclay picked out the moment we shook hands.

"Zoey, could you pull the Leland House file, please?" I ask in my no-nonsense professional woman voice.

Zoey sets two cups of coffee on the desk and sighs her third futile sigh of the morning. "You're holding the Leland House file, Dolores."

"So I am," I say, and give my sweetest smile to Austin Barclay.

After coffee, in the Buick on the way to Tryon Street, Austin asks me whether I have been in Woodland always.

"Not Woodland—Sacramento. I went to school in the East, then came back to do graduate work."

"In business?"

"No." I turn to gauge his reaction. "Not business. Literature."

He doesn't show surprise, and he doesn't come out with the "Guess I better watch my grammar" line that, for me, turns the most alluring human prospects into despicable morons. He is watching the trees and yards as I drive. His profile is sturdy, his dark eyes heavy lashed. He is a nice-looking man, and I wonder why he is single, why he has left New York, why he wants a rundown old house.

I take Tryon Street slowly. Virtually all the homes on the street are recently gentrified Victorian, and each has its own special attraction. My reasoning behind the slow pass-by is to provide the visual evidence that the neighborhood is upscale, single-family, and worth the daunting investment of time and money that restoration requires. When I pull up to the Leland House, Austin Barclay smiles again.

"Nice neighborhood. This is what I had in mind, so far, anyway."

I remember that this is a test, that I am an honest realtor.

"The house needs loads and loads of work, inside and out, but it would be worth it, you can imagine its potential by looking at the others." I push the sagging picket gate along the uneven brick pathway with the toe of my pump. Austin brushes by me to lift the gate and swing it open. I remind myself to prune the exaggerated praise.

We stand for a moment in the yard. The remains of a sack of steer manure have spilled across the bricks, and I have left a hand shovel and a shaggy pile of drying weeds at the base of the porch steps.

"Is someone still keeping the garden up?" Austin asks.

"I—uh—I come here sometimes, after work, to water," I say. "The house has been on the market for a good while, and I've gotten sort of interested in the flowers . . . there are so many—"

"They're beautiful," he says. He wraps a hand around the trunk of the trumpet vine that twines up the porch balustrade. "Campsis."

He is talking to himself, not to me, so I can stare at his broad back as he gingerly takes the porch steps, two at a time.

"Mr. Barclay?"

He turns at the top of the stairs. "You can call me Austin, Ms. Meredith."

"It's Dolores," I say. "Do you like the yard? Are you thinking of pulling this out and putting down roll-out lawn?"

He is bent over the plywood that covers the broken panes of the front door. He pulls a screwdriver from his rear pocket and pries the plywood gently from the door frame. "Not in a thousand years. Your flowers are safe with me." He is grinning now.

My best-laid plans are going awry here. I climb the porch steps, careful with my heels. "What are you doing?"

"I wanted to see if the glass is beveled." He gently leans the plywood against the porch railing so the pink spray-painted letters reading BOBBY DOES ELENA stand upside down.

"See here?" He points to the edges of the two remaining panes.

"This can be hard to match—sometimes it's easier to replace every pane than to find a match. But it's sure nice old glass."

"But you haven't even seen the interior . . . don't you think you ought to—"

"I'll put it back if I don't take the house. Don't worry—Bobby and Elena will never suspect a thing."

This makes me blush, so it's a good moment to open the lockbox and go through the motions of unlocking the front door. I can see that I won't have to narrate this walk-through. Mr. Austin Barclay is completely capable of detecting the Leland House's most minute flaws entirely by himself. As I follow him into the entryway, I have the most curious feeling that the examinee has become the examiner, and I wonder whether I am passing or failing.

I trail him into the front room, the parlor, really, and watch him kneel to peer up into the chimney. He scrapes at the sooty brick with the screwdriver. When he pulls back from the flue, he has a smudge of soot on his temple. I turn away, spy a Dixie cup half-filled with red wine settled precariously on the windowsill, and decide not to tell him about the soot.

I am pouring the wine down the kitchen drain when Austin emerges from the pantry.

"This is great—they've vented through the floor and through the ceiling for cold storage. I'll bet the closets upstairs are lined with cedar, too."

He is so boyishly happy with the prospects of this house that I can't resist asking him whether he is really, truly a lawyer.

"Yep," he answers. "Late of Vickers and Mallory, Corporate Law, New York City. But no more—from now on I'm an absent-minded professor."

"How do you know so much about houses? You didn't learn this stuff in New York City, did you?"

"It may seem like too-perfect poetic resolution, but no, I didn't learn this stuff in the city. I learned it here, in Woodland, when I was a kid. I worked as a journeyman carpenter for Billy Day. And my dad knew a lot about building, too."

"Will you miss the city? Woodland is about as far from cosmopolitan as one gets."

"Not only will I not miss the city, I will relish the simple town life. That's why I didn't want to stay in Davis—too urban."

"You must be having a classic midlife change," I tease him.

He turns from the wainscoting where he has traced a pattern in dust.

"Some kind of change, anyway. I don't know about classic."

We tramp upstairs, where Austin checks the view from every window and pushes open the attic door with a broom handle. He sees the house for what it is—for what it could be, and he seems pleased with every feature, every flaw.

I hold the plywood against the front door so Austin can reset the nails.

"This is the first improvement that I'm making," he says, returning the nails into the holes in the plywood with the spade end of my hand shovel.

"You're buying a hammer?" I ask.

"I'm fixing this glass. You can let go now." He stands up and brushes his hands against his Levi's. "You, Ms. Meredith, have made a sale today."

I reach up to rub the sooty patch on his temple.

"You, Mr. Barclay, have soot on your forehead."

CHAPTER FOUR

I taste a liquor never brewed——

ᦞ

I taste a liquor never brewed—
From Tankards scooped in Pearl—
Not all the Vats upon the Rhine
Yield such an Alcohol!

Inebriate of Air—am I—
And Debauchee of Dew—
Reeling—thro endless summer days—
From inns of Molten Blue—

When "Landlords" turn the drunken Bee
Out of the Foxglove's door—
When Butterflies—renounce their "drams"—
I shall but drink the more!

Till Seraphs swing their snowy Hats—
And Saints—to windows run—
To see the little Tippler
Leaning against the—Sun—

EMILY DICKINSON 1860

RICK DAY AND I offload the doug fir two-by-fours fast, leveraging eight of them at once against the U-Haul's tailgate and swinging them onto the Leland House porch. It is midmorning and hot. Rick works hard, as his grandfather did, talking little, grunting every time he hefts a load of lumber against his hip, backwalking up the porch steps without breaking his stride. He is careful to step over the lobelia, which is trailing across the brick walkway, a consideration Dolores Meredith would like to hear, I think. Rick drives nails like a third-generation carpenter should; with his help, the new framing of the interior walls of the first floor is nearly done. He is almost a man, and at noon when we break for lunch he unscrews the lid of a Mason jar filled with iced tea and says that a beer sure would be nice.

There are some bottles in the ice chest inside, I tell him.

No, he says, he has ball practice after he finishes with me. "It don't work so well to drink midday," he says with a practiced discipline that recalls something of my father. "Makes a guy want to siesta instead of frame walls."

He is wise; I pass on the beer as well. Inside the house, it is still cool, and tented piles of sawdust perfume the air with the sweet promise of newly sawn lumber. The contractor laid the new subflooring and set the roof trusses last week. As soon as his crew lays the roof, it will be just Rick and I and the finish work. I anticipate the transformation from job site to home, when the Leland House will empty of hired hands and settle into its character: the walls of the place in which I will live. Now they shelter collapsed Pepsi cans and twenty-pound boxes of sinkers and bales of insulation and sawhorses and cigarette butts, but I can see them stripped bare, repainted and restained, the windows framing the leafy outline of the centuried elms on Tryon Street. A pyramid of boxes is standing where I imagine the sofa will sit. I was right to leave most of my furniture—streamlined pale Danish stuff—in the New York apartment: it wouldn't suit the house, which wants dark wood against the polished oak floors.

At two-thirty, after he has swept up and coiled his chalk line, I tell Rick to take off a half hour early. "Have a siesta," I kid him. He gives me a rare smile, a handshake, and heads down the porch steps out to the street, where a freckled redhead is waiting for him in the passenger seat of his old Chevy.

"You could have asked her in," I call after him.

He stops and shakes his head. "Stace knows better." But I see him reach over to kiss her when he slides behind the wheel. She waves to me as the old car's engine turns over once, twice, and they are gone.

I work for another hour sanding the wainscoting in the parlor. Beneath the layers of chalky paint—even pale pink at one strata—I find the whorls of a dark mahogany paneling. With a flat satin finish, the wood will glow against the morning sun or the light cast by a soft bulb. Above the wainscoting trim, I can envision a lightly patterned wallpaper, simple lines flecked with dark blue. I sit back on my heels, pull the dust mask from my face, and tell myself I will have to start hunting old pieces for this room.

From the porch come footfalls, shuffling but deliberate, and I wonder if Rick has left his lunchbox. I turn at the tap on the glass pane of the front door. An old man stands there. Despite the heat, he wears a thready wool suitcoat, forty years old at least, and rests his hand on the marbled head of a cane.

He studies me when I pull open the door, which scratches across the floor. I will have to reset the hinges soon to save both the door and the floor from all the comings and goings of rebuilding.

"Need to rehang that, son. That or plane off the bottom. Course the lintel could be sagging some." He steps through the door, although I haven't said a word, and extends a hand knotted by arthritis. "Trevor Tuskes. Pleased to meet you. We are somewhat neighbors."

"Austin Barclay. Pleased to meet you, Mr. Tuskes." He holds my hand beyond the shake, as if he is reading the new calluses on my palm.

He struggles with something in the stretched pocket of his jacket.

"Here." He extends a crumpled brown lunch bag to me. "By way of housewarming. Seen what you're doing here, thought you might appreciate this. Myself, I replaced with new."

I unwrap the bag and find a doorknob, not so tarnished that

the ornate pattern stamped on the brass handle is indecipherable. There seems to be a circle of flowers twined around the swell of the knob, the blooms so delicate they could be forget-me-nots.

"What a beaut . . . come on in. It's not quite home in here yet . . . Can I get you something, a beer?"

But he's already hobbled to the edge of the porch, where he surveys the tangled thicket of yard. "She put them anemones down, did she." He swings his cane toward a nest of foliage beyond the porch railing. "She's a good girl, that one is."

He doesn't hear my farewell, or he chooses not to answer, and I stand holding the doorknob to my chest, watching his slow procession up Tryon Street.

The doorknob is on my mind the next morning, when I drive from the Hacienda Motel to Meredith Realty to sign closing papers. The sellers were generous about allowing work on the house before the deed recorded, but I haven't taken the final liberty of sleeping there overnight, although the idea of putting down a chaise mattress and a sleeping bag in one of the newly sheetrocked rooms upstairs has sorely tempted me every evening as I returned to my king-size bed and large TV screen in Room 242, where the nightly serial visitors to the permanent resident in 245 made me question whether I ought to have picked a motel so close to the freeway. In my hurry to flee the Hacienda, I emptied a month's dirty laundry into the backseat of the Jeep and piled on top of that four law books, a brand-new finish hammer, and a backpack I had ordered by phone on my second day in Woodland. Lupe would fly from New York City in a moment if she could see the jumbled haste with which I checked out of the motel, but something tells me that Dolores Meredith won't bat an eye at the cargo I carry. What was it Trevor Tuskes had said . . . anemones? The doorknob is safely nestled inside the nail pouch of my carpenter's belt, hanging on the pantry door in the Leland House. I wish that I had brought it with me to show Dolores, to ask her about Trevor and the anemones.

I park behind the Volvo, fish inside two briefcases before I locate a checkbook, and walk to the realty. As I push open the glass door, the tableau inside holds me for a moment. Dolores has her bare feet up on her desk, her arms around her knees. Zoey is unusually animated, alternating between pointing her finger at Dolores and pantomiming pulling her hair out from her scalp. Their heads turn when I push through the door. Legs swing off the desk, arms fall to sides.

"Hello, Austin," they chime.

"Am I interrupting something? I can always swing back in an hour," I say.

"No, no, come on in," Dolores says, and disappears beneath her desk to locate her sandals.

"Coffee?" says Zoey, returned to normality.

"I know yours beats the Hacienda Motel's," I smile at her.

"Sit down, Mr. Barclay." Dolores waves her arm vaguely. "The paperwork is all set, and Zoey, our neighborhood notary and resident coffee fetcher, is ready to do her duty." She sticks her tongue out at Zoey's turned back.

"You've had *your* quota this morning already," Zoey snipes.

One by one, we leaf through the escrow papers. I sign my name wherever Dolores has red-checked a blank line.

"For a man of the law, you don't," the phone on her desk rings, "read your contracts too carefully," she admonishes. The phone rings again, and she excuses herself to answer.

"Dolores Meredith here." A long pause. "Sweetie, it doesn't have to rhyme . . . well, if you want it to, then it does matter . . . *Goat? Boat? Shoat?* Kind of a baby pig . . . I think." She raises her eyebrows at me.

I mouth yes to her. *"Moat? Throat? Tote? Croak?"* I try helping.

"Jorge, how about *croak?* Like frogs?" Dolores mutes thanks to me, says good-bye to Jorge.

"Your son?" I ask her.

"An ideal candidate, but no, not my son. My . . . student, sort of." She checks my last signature and tells Zoey it's time for action.

Zoey notarizes the papers with a flourish, giving Dolores one hard stare after she shakes the stack straight and collects stamped envelopes. "I'm running these over to First American," she says. "Do you require my services any longer?"

"No. Great, Zoe. Thanks." Dolores misses, or ignores, Zoey's sarcasm and reaches across the desk to shake my hand. "It's a done deal now. I can't present you with the keys because you are already in possession, Mr. Barclay." Her hand is warm and strong, but she slips it from mine before I release my fingers. It feels unfinished, this too-quick handshake, and if Zoey weren't knocking about at her desk I would say as much to Dolores.

Zoey steps through the door. Dolores and I watch her trot down the sidewalk until she is out of view.

"I was wondering—"

"I thought we might—"

We laugh, and I offer, "Ladies first."

"No," she says, eyes downcast, "clients are always first."

"I'm not a client anymore, but I'll take my cue. I thought we might have dinner Friday. To celebrate. My finding the house, your selling it?"

She looks at me dead straight. Her eyes are blue-green. She winds a curl of tawny hair around her finger.

"That would be, Mr. Barclay," she says, a perfect reading, "just lovely."

By the end of the week, jeans and a wrinkled dress shirt are the cleanest clothes I can find in the impossible confusion I have made in the Leland House. And the cranky plumbing of the single bathroom shower doused me first with pure hot water, then pure cold. To excuse the fact that I've not made reservations (I wouldn't have known where), I confess my housekeeping when Dolores meets me at the door of her apartment, an enormous gray cat caught up under her arm, and gives my worn Levi's the once-over. She thrusts the cat in my arms and disappears through the door to a kitchenette.

"I'm running a little late here, so if you hold Milton, we'll be even." She calls above the sound of running water, "You look like you're dressed for western . . . Can you do sawdust on the floor and country swing?"

"I'm an expert at sawdust on the floor, ma'am," I call back to her and then say more softly to the cat, "I don't know about country swing." He twitches his tail. I'm pretty good at reading body language, so I let him slide slowly onto the rumpled afghan that's taking up most of the couch.

"Was Milton polite?" Dolores says, touching my back.

She is not beautiful, this unusual woman, but there is something to her that I recognize even though I can't name it, can't assign the accurate adjective to capture her bold eccentricities, her sudden kindnesses, her unpredictable but satisfying words. She has pulled her hair back severely from her forehead—it's tap water that has temporarily tamed the natural curls—and she wears little makeup that I can detect. She is, as I am, on the brink of middle age, so that what passes for youth on cursory inspection stands up to closer scrutiny as the more intriguing complexity of maturity. I am entirely at home here in her untidy apartment with her oversize cat. I am also staring.

"He didn't scratch you, did he?" she asks, all seriousness.

"He's been a gentleman. You look very nice."

"I *am* very nice, on balance. And so is Milton, when he's not protecting his territory."

"Paradise?" I say, sounding too clever by half, even to myself.

A half-smile disappears. "Not lately . . . Milts, hold down the fort." She strokes the old tabby, who rolls himself onto his back, paws in air. "He must approve of you. That's the surrender position there."

Dolores guides me through Woodland, south to Gibson Road, then west where the subdivisions cease and valley farmhouses sit on dirt-bare squares centered in the graph line furrows of tomatoes, corn, peppers, and beans. The windows of the Jeep are down, generating breeze with the damp heavy smell of irrigated loam.

"Do you want the air conditioner?" I turn to look at Dolores, who has trapped her hair with one hand to keep it from blowing.

"Never," she says, then explains. "Farms have never made me want to roll up the windows. There was a dairy farm in Roseville we used to drive past on our way up to the mountains, summers when I was a kid, and my father would tell us, 'Smell them roses,' as if we were in Kew Gardens." She tips her head back and breathes deeply. "I think sometimes we learn to prefer or to disdain, even at the sensory level, because we were taught to, so early on."

Roses remind me of anemones.

"An older man name of Trevor Tuskes said something about some anemones in the garden . . ."

"Oh, you've met Trevor!" She claps her hands. "He has been watching guard over that house since we put up the sale sign. He's a gardener, vegetables mostly. He lives around the corner from you in a little bungalow with black trim. The anemones must be flowering—" She catches her breath. "Can I come see them—the blooms? Have you been watering?"

I laugh. "You really want to snoop around for roll-out lawn, don't you? Of course you can come by." I recount the progress we make daily, Rick Day and the trailing lobelia.

Zeke's Dance Palace and Restaurant is a ramshackle wooden barn that has continually sprouted extensions, Dolores narrates, for forty years since Zeke returned from France and vowed to establish an all-American bar for all-American veterans. The "and Restaurant" is a precarious cedar-lined room that bridges the slough at Birds' Landing, and the blinking green lights of the neon sign on the highway advertise DINING ON THE WATER. When the waitress, a skinny kid in loose black jeans and a sequined western shirt, seats us, we can't see the water. But I feel the current, a slow-moving, shadowed swell of water, its calm surface deceitful. Some low-down and mournful George Jones wails in the bar.

Dolores turns the white plastic carnation in the wine bottle substituting for a vase. "I'm fond of Zeke's," she says, pulling the flower from the bottle and studying its petals. "And since you were dressed the part, it seemed the right choice. You don't mind, do you? It's not New York—"

"It's fine. I'm not complaining—not even thinking about too much except that it's been a long time since I've danced to George Jones—"

"What! No line dancing on the East Coast?" She drops the carnation.

"No dancing on the East Coast."

"All work and no play?"

"Pretty close . . . it's part of what brought me back."

"That you wanted to work less?"

"That I wanted to live more."

The waitress, Loelle her name tag reads, leans across our table to light a thick, half-melted red candle. "Sorry. And your utensils." She slides checkered napkins and forks and knives across our place mats. "You want to wait to order? I'll be back in a jif."

Dolores winks at her. "We'll be fine, sweetie. We have time." She picks up the carnation, pretends to smell it, and sets it down again. "It's the plague of the baby boomers, isn't it?"

I wait for her to explain.

"We're hitting forty and wondering if we overlooked something along the way . . . bypassed our bliss or something—"

"You're a Joseph Campbell fan?"

"Sort of. The bliss part, I think. You?"

"What he says about the landscape . . . the sacred places geography gives us, I believe that . . . yes."

"Your sacred places?"

"The Sierra Nevada, for sure. He says we can find our stations of bliss in books, even."

"I buy that. Or used to . . ." Dolores is twirling an escaped strand of hair again. A sliver of a scab lines her forefinger.

She hides her hands in her lap. "Why, really really why, did you give up New York to come back to this town?"

I know the answer to this question in my bones and blood, in the feel of the hand plane against the wood banister in the Leland

House, but I am not sure I can put it into words so she will understand. This is important to me, that she understand.

I start slow. "I can't describe it as a conscious decision, although it ended up being that. For a couple of years, my life hasn't—hasn't fit, exactly. It was comfortable, but chafing in some kind of subconscious way. It was as if the—joys of daily life, I guess—were leaching away." I lighten up. "Something called me back to Woodland . . . The mountains? The Leland House? My station of bliss?"

She smiles. The flickering candlelight changes her hair from gold to brown and back again. "Sometimes . . . something can work perfectly one day and be all wrong the next. . . . You wake up one day and realize certain people in your life have been terribly miscast . . . and you start to forget your own lines . . ."

"Do you miss him now?" I am guessing.

She is not startled by my surmise. "Not at all. That's the scary part . . . the not missing? It makes me wonder about myself . . . whether *I'm* missing some piece, some part?"

Loelle returns with menus, but Dolores hands them back and tells her we'll have the catfish platters—what else on the river delta—and orders two Heinekens as well. She returns to her missing piece theory.

"And you, Austin? No little woman in New York waiting for your call, ready to fly out west at the drop of a hat?" Under her teasing tones there's a serious inquiry.

"Not a one." I lift the frosted bottle of beer Loelle has set in front of me. I'd like to roll it across my temples the way Rick Day cooled his brow with a can of Coke yesterday. I feel as I haven't felt since I was Rick's age: the slow burn beneath the laden teasing that tells me this is a girl with whom I want to talk for hours into the night, a woman whom I want to pull against my chest to savor the beating of her heart.

"And no story? I told you mine."

"I believe you just delivered the abridged version. My story is so boring and so predictable you don't even want to hear it."

"No divorced wives, no clamoring children in the background?"

"Not a one."

"Why, then?"

"I could ask the same of you, couldn't I?"

"My answer would be that the right person never came along."

"Mine too. The cosmic plan has failed me there." I turn the beer bottle in the damp ring it has made on the tablecloth. Loelle sets the platters of catfish in front of us. I study the round lumps on the side of the slabs of fish.

"Hush puppies. Zeke's wife's own recipe. They're hell on cholesterol levels."

"We'll dance it off, won't we?"

We do. There is real sawdust on the Dance Palace floor. I am clumsy, but Dolores is patient. She teaches me to follow the booted, swirling couples who dip and swing. Before long, we are lined up with them, promenading and swirling partners. The band shifts into low gear: the lead singer croons "Apartment Number Nine," a number one hit by Tammy Wynette back in the sixties, popular among the football-playing cowboys at Woodland High, who would shout out the lyrics in falsetto against the bass acoustics of the shower stalls in the men's locker room. Dolores puts her hands on my shoulders, leans her head against my chest. She hums with the lead guitar. I trace my palms down her spine and cinch them around her waist. I don't have trouble following the beat, and our feet slide across the dusty floor in a western waltz.

When the music ends, one long wailing note of the slide guitar, she looks up and says, Texas-style, "Why Mr. Barclay, you didn't step on my little toes even once!" and pulls me to the bar.

We are driven to leave our beers half full on the bar top by a staccato-voiced, silver-haired temptress who finagles "Achey Breaky Heart" out of the lead singer. At the first chords, we turn to each other in laughing disgust. Shaking her head, Dolores takes my hand and pulls me through the smoky, stomping throng into the night.

Outside the Dance Palace, she turns to me. "I have a limited tolerance level for certain forms of country western."

I laugh with her, the hooting and hollering inside Zeke's a canned wall of sound in the night. "Your tolerance level is my tolerance level. Point zero on that one."

The delta breeze lifts Dolores's damp hair from her neck. We stand and study the slough, whose muddy dark waters run silent in the summer night. We are silent, too, in the cool-down after dancing. I unlock the Jeep's door for Dolores.

"Recovered from those hush puppies?"

I press my hand against my rib cage. "It's my heart," I say, "all that deep-fry just larded up there in the very heart of my heart."

She laughs and slips inside the Jeep.

The engine hums on the drive back to Woodland.

When we are back on the lit streets of town, I break the quiet. "Who is Jorge?"

"Oh, Jorge . . ." She looks out the window. "Jorge Mendoza is a second-grader with whom I am falling desperately in love."

"And?"

"I'm volunteering at the Hispanic Community Center, doing afternoon poetry workshops with the children of migrant workers. Jorge is special—he doesn't need prodding? And he writes the most wonderful poems in the sternest rhyme schemes imaginable—"

"The croaking shoat in the moat?"

"Yes, that . . . he's taken to calling me almost daily, sometimes when I think he's supposed to be in school . . . I've only met his father. It might be that there's no mama in the picture."

"I'll bet you work wonders with them, the kids."

"Not wonders. I keep wanting them to fly into free verse, but they are sticklers for rhyme and rhythm. I had to ask Eddie to order a rhyming dictionary for me after the second class. My mind doesn't seem to work in rhymes . . ."

"Could I come in and watch you one day?"

I pull up to a vacant four-way stop. Dolores turns to look at me, her face a mockery of horror. "Such an intimate request for the first date! Only if you'll help! You'd have to sign a contract, of course."

"Of course. We'll make it as legal as humanly possible."

In front of Dolores's apartment, we sit on the curb. The town is solemn, the air a soothing balm. She studies the scab on her finger. A childlike gesture, it prompts me to ask how her English major evolved into a career in real estate.

"The sad truth is . . . I realized I wasn't a gifted writer. Capable, yes. Well educated, yes. The practical answer is that one has to take up something, right? It was almost accidental, the way it happened. I fell into the business; I've never fallen out. Oh, I guess I just didn't have the guts. It takes guts, you know. To write in a blind, to stake such high hopes on the unknown."

She stands up suddenly and extends her hand. "I should be going in. Milton will be on patrol, for sure."

"It's been swell," I say, and rise to my feet. "You'll come by to inspect the anemones?"

"Sure. And poetry class is Wednesday afternoons. Just call, when you know you're coming."

"I'll do that." Dolores two-steps down the walk to her apartment door.

As I step around the Jeep, she sings out in Tammy Wynette's twang:

> *"Inebriate of Air—am I—*
> *And Debauchee of Dew—"*

I hold my arms up to the sky and answer her:

> *"Reeling—thro endless summer days—*
> *From inns of Molten Blue—"*

She marches from her apartment door to the streetside, arms swinging. "Mr. Austin Barclay," she shouts, "you are a surprising man."

CHAPTER FIVE

Did the harebell loose her girdle —

꧁꧂

Did the Harebell loose her girdle
To the lover Bee
Would the Bee the Harebell hallow
Much as formerly?

Did the "Paradise"—persuaded—
Yield her moat of pearl—
Would the Eden be an Eden,
Or the Earl—an Earl?

EMILY DICKINSON 1860

JORGE DOES NOT leave my side. As soon as I enter the Hispanic Community Center on Wednesday afternoon, he becomes my second self. He slips his soiled fingers into mine and shadows me around the classroom until the dirt from his little palm is caked into my hand, too. I offer him my Magic Markers. His doe brown eyes widen at the prospect of uncapping the thick-tipped pens, whose caustic scent he inhales before lining them up neatly on the children's table. To my wicker basket of scavengered poem starters he has contributed his own artifacts. Last week he brought in three wooden thread spools, painted a gruesome blue-black and glued solidly together, end to end. Today it is a rusty one-clawed hammer head, which Jorge positions in the basket, reconsiders, and then restores to his own pocket.

The other children eat brownies and kick their sandaled feet against the table legs. Their first poems, illustrated, hang at child level around the walls of the classroom, where they like to point to their names and read their lines, more from memory, I think, than from their cursory connection to English-language phonetics. Though their spelling is often surprising, the children have musical ears. When they gulp the dregs of their milk and settle onto the oval carpet that marks our arena, I read to them from Ogden Nash. They collapse in giggles at his lines, which inspire a spate of silly word pairs, offered to me with a high-pitched, near hysterical excitement.

Soria has chocolate frosting on her cheek. I am trying to wipe it clean with a dampened napkin.

"You're a squirmy worm," I tell her, tickling her stomach with the wet paper.

She falls back against the rug and shrieks, "No, *you're* a squirmy worm!"

Jorge throws his arms around my neck. "Dolores is a cake snake!"

"Dolores *makes* the cake snakes," I tell him when he presses his cheek against mine. "She makes them for you, you funny bunny."

Soria freezes. Jorge's arms tighten. I turn to follow their stares to the open door where Austin is standing, a half-smile on his lips.

He walks to our rug and kneels.

"Is this the poetry class?" he asks, face-to-face with Alma.

Alma squints at me, her face expressionless. I wink at her. "It's okay," I mouth.

"Jorge said Dolores is a cake snake!" she shrills at Austin.

"And who might you be?" I ask him, eyebrows raised.

"If Jorge's a funny bunny," he says, "and you are the cake snake, then I must be . . . the house mouse? The loose moose? The legal eagle?"

I laugh. Two beats behind me, the children laugh. Austin captures their attention. By the end of class, they are cuddled in his lap or hanging on his shoulders, smitten by his willingness to play their games and, as I am, entranced by his easy good humor.

Jorge is the last to leave, trailing on his father's hand, deciding at the last minute to unveil his hammer head to Austin, who is properly appreciative.

"You've won them over," I tell him, picking up the red plastic mugs on which I have printed the children's names. He tosses crumpled napkins one at a time into the garbage pail.

"I like what you're doing," he tells me, bending to clean up a shot that has rebounded. He turns and looks at me. "I like that you do this."

His compliment, simple and straight, warms me. Austin recognizes this fragment of myself that I have only just discovered, a vital part separate from bottom lines and profit margins, ghostly and gossamer still in my own reflection. The only other man I've ever known who might have offered me such praise is my father, who expected his children to seek small ways to right what we found wrong with the world. Austin's capacity to speak these words—words which aren't, finally, about us at all—brings him close, closer than I ever came to Henry Talmouth.

I juggle crayons from one hand to the other. "Thanks for coming by. The kids will have a whole new regard for the animal kingdom after hearing your rhymes . . . I won't know what to follow with for next week . . ."

"Vegetables and minerals?"

"Not bad—I might do that."

We walk out to the cars. I toss the grocery bag of plastic cups through the Volvo's open window and turn to Austin.

"I thought, if you're willing, we might have dinner again," he says.

The afternoon sunlight grants a sheen to his dark hair. I'd like to run my hand through the loose strands the way I might Jorge's, to feel the sun-soaked texture of his curls.

"Dinner? When?" I say, jerking my hand back from the Volvo's door handle, raised to egg-frying temperatures by the valley heat.

Austin reaches inside the door and opens it.

"Get in and I'll shut it for you. How about Saturday? Seven?"

"Seven's fine."

Austin stands back from the Volvo. I rest my elbow on the window frame and wince when the baked metal touches my arms. Austin shakes his head, a dismayed frown on his face.

"Austin?"

He leans to the window, careful not to touch the frame.

"I appreciate that you've never said a word about my car . . . the apartment . . . even Zoey doesn't let up—"

"It's something else I like about you, Dolores," he says, and then he is kissing me, quick and off-target, on the corner of my mouth.

At lunch Thursday, Zoey arranges her meal in a tidy place setting on my desk, which I have cleared of mail and price listings. She sets out stair step Tupperware containers, a sandwich neatly creased into a tinfoil envelope, and an insulated glass of iced tea.

In front of me sit a forlorn orange, a nonfat yogurt, and a diet Pepsi from the machine at the neighboring travel agency.

"What's the special today?" I say wistfully, watching her open the Tupperwares.

"Sliced peaches, baby carrots, ranch dressing, turkey salad—with extra celery—and Good Earth Original." She handles each item as she identifies it, first framing it with two hands, like a flight attendant demonstrating the escape routes from a 747.

I give her my most timid beseeching look.

"Dolores," she says, disgustedly handing over half the turkey salad sandwich, "if you would just get yourself organized for *once* you could do this too, you know."

"It's really good, Zoe," I say, chewing. "You make a darn good turkey salad sandwich."

She hmmphs and takes a dainty bite of peach from her spork.

"Actually, I did all the food preparation I could handle yesterday baking those brownies for my little poets."

Zoe sets down the peaches and applauds.

"Scratch or package?"

"Oh come on, Zoe! Package with melted chocolate chips for frosting. And they weren't overcooked. The kids ate them, no complaints."

"They're going well then, the classes?"

"We may not be winning Pulitzers, but we're happy."

"Did you find anything for the Walters yet?" she asks, snapping the lid of the largest Tupperware, moving to the new topic as if it's the next course of her lunch.

"I think they're going to decide on one of the four-bedroom Brookside models. She got all misty-eyed about the felt wallpaper in the kitchen, and the optional RV pad made his day. He kept pacing the side yard up and over, measuring in feet and then yards. I was waiting for him to do it in meters."

I take a sip of my Pepsi. "Yep, old Phil was positively and unabridgedly thrilled by the notion that he could park his yet unpurchased recreational vehicle in a location where the whole neighborhood could see it twenty-four hours a day."

I begin to peel my orange.

"You don't know that . . . it's unkind of you to assume character flaws about everyone you deal with . . . you make your living off these people, Dolores."

"Not everyone. Don't wave your spork at me. Just the ones who drive around sixty thousand dollars worth of automobile intending for the neighbors to take notice. And it's not unkind, it's true. Ostentation is unforgivable. It says so in the Bible, the Koran, and the Talmud. So there."

Zoey shakes her head and reaches for a segment of my orange.

"I noticed a certain recent customer is driving a pretty hot Jeep these days." She thinks she is sly, does Zoey.

"That Jeep is the first car a certain customer has owned in twenty years," I retort.

Zoey pushes the carrot Tupperware toward me, follows it with the dressing: an invitation to girl talk.

"He's wonderful, Zoe. He may be the most remarkable man I've ever met." I lean forward on my arms. "He can recite obscure

Emily Dickinson. The children adore him. He owns a backpack—do you know how hard it is to find a man who owns a backpack these days?"

Zoey looks doubtful. "And he has no interest in RV pads?"

"Zoe, I'm dead serious. He knows the Latin name for *trumpet vine,* for God's sake. And you should see what he's done to the Leland House—"

"I have. You were right there—he is doing it justice. And I guessed he was the reason you've been so . . . frisky lately." Zoey sips from her iced Good Earth.

I wait for more. Despite our incessant culture clashes, Zoey is my closest friend. Her judgments do matter to me. I am even willing to confess to her that my seven-year attachment to Henry Talmouth was a bloody blunder—an assertion she has held in edited opinion from the beginning.

Zoey continues, finding her way. "I watched you do this once before, if you'll recall, Dolo. I'm getting a kind of déjà vu feeling here? And since I seem to be the only voice of reason in your immediate circle, I recommend more caution than you are showing."

"You like him, don't you?"

"Henry? Never!"

"Not Henry. Austin. You do like him?"

Zoey lays her hand on mine. Her voice is soft. "I'm thinking of you. Your expectations are so unreasonable, Dolores. Your ideal of happiness might be unreachable. I listen to you satirize the Walters and the Penningtons and the Peraltas as they troop through here looking for their own bliss—don't scoff!—and I think you're setting yourself up. I think"—Zoey seems to pray into her tented hands—"I think sometimes you doom yourself with your own standards. Do you understand what I'm saying?"

For some reason which I will figure out, her words remind me of those of Dr. Chalmers. I feel the same adamant refusal welling up in my tight throat that I did when he passed me my manuscript of poems and went on to tell me that he thought, with his recommendation, I could find a teaching position at one of the local colleges. I never picked up the letters he wrote for me. Less than a week after the graduate school ceremonies, I was working at Parker, Aubrey, and Downes. I read contracts instead of poetry and designed a world so far removed from my creative disappointment that it could have been on another planet.

Zoey is waiting for me to say that I understand, that I'll be good.

"I am trying to be realistic here," I say meekly. "I think we're compatible, is what I think. Is that too much to expect?"

Zoey pats my hand. "Of course not. Compatibility is a bare minimum requirement. Even Tammy and Phil Walters insist on that. Felt flowers and RV pads are simply compatibility on their scale."

That evening in my tiny patio, with Milton settled into my lap and the paper folded back to the editorial page, I study what Zoey said to me about compatibility. I think about Daddy and Todd and me, the snug fit of the comfortable love we had for each other throughout my growing up. I wonder about my mother, whom I never knew and Todd claims not to recall, about the way Daddy would glow when he began one of his stories: "Now your mother . . ." I remember her fragile tea set, her silver—so unlike me!—and try to envision the pairing between her refined delicacy and Daddy's clumsy, expansive enthusiasm. I think about Zoey and her husband, Ted, both so commonsensical and calm, devoted to each other without histrionics. I think about Henry Talmouth and his country club wife, Ellen, and see that perhaps he has stayed with her for fifteen years because of something even more binding than the welfare of their children. I think about Phil and Tammy Walters, their adoration of each other's bald needs and bad taste. Maybe Zoey is right, maybe there is a missing element in the inflexible equation to which I have pledged myself.

Milton stretches in my lap. The phone rings. I consider letting the machine pick up, then think better and slide Milton onto the ground and step into the kitchenette, where my bare feet stick to the cool linoleum. It is Austin, who needs advice on picking a place for dinner on Saturday. I suggest to him Old Sacramento, on the river perhaps. He tells me about the wallpapering—he's decided to contract it—but he is sanding the floors himself. And the soaker hoses are running in the front garden, too, he adds. I laugh. He tells me he will be scheduling a physical and setting up his office in the law school next week.

"Are you quiet tonight, or am I imagining?" he asks.

"You're not imagining. I'm quiet."

"I'll let you go."

"I'm thinking . . . I've been studying the couples I know . . ."

"And?"

"I'm still studying."

"I'll let you go. I know serious research when I see it. I'll make reservations in town for eight. See you at seven."

I hold the phone for a moment after Austin hangs up. I can hear my heartbeats, heavy thuds against the wall of my chest. Milton stands against the kitchen screen, wanting in.

"Okay, Milts," I tell him, "okay."

I am still studying as I drive to the office Saturday morning. I am meeting Dodie and Frank Murphy, neighbors from my growing-up years in Sacramento. They have stayed in the old neighborhood until the infirmities of age rendered the steep stairs and the sweeping lawns impossible for them; now they want to get out of town into something smaller, single-story, on a slow street. I remember Dodie's roses: great climbing masses of yellow and pink that reached up the shingled side of their house to the third-floor windows. In summer and again in late fall, Frank dragged out an extension ladder, leaned it against the house, and trimmed his way up the thorny trellis, clipping the bulbed spent blossoms. And every summer and late fall, Dodie would dance about the base of the ladder, calling up to Frank to watch his step, be careful, dear, take it slow. It's okay, Mother, he would chorus back to her, just watch my feet.

Once I gathered up the rose hips that showered beneath the ladder and presented a bucket of them to Dodie, who exclaimed over my hard work and promised me we would make jelly. We did make the jelly, twenty pint jars of perfumed amber. At ten I probably wasn't much help in Dodie's kitchen, but I can recollect the tone of voice Dodie used to caution me about the steamy pots of boiling water, the hot glass of the sterilized Mason jars: it was the same tone with which she sang out her protective blessings to Frank during his twice yearly expeditions up the side of the house. It's been two years since I've seen them, and helping them with their move is something I look forward to.

The Buick is on the street, the listings I have in mind are neatly clipped into a folder labeled MURPHY by the time Dodie and Frank pull up before the realty in their immaculate Ford Falcon. I run to the curb to greet them.

"Hello you two!"

Frank steps nimbly out of the Ford and offers his cheek to my lips.

"Now, Dolores, let me get Mother out here so she can say a real hello."

I help Frank lift Dodie from her seat.

She laughs. "I can get in all right, it's the getting out that fools me!" She reaches her arms around me and plants a powdery, lilacky kiss on my cheek. "How is my little neighbor girl?"

"Hoping to be your neighbor again soon," I tell her, and sling her bag over my shoulder.

She takes hold of one of my arms and one of Frank's. We move slowly to the Buick door where, good to her word, Dodie slips into the passenger side without any help.

I tell Dodie and Frank that I want to show them some houses that have two baths and two entrances. Without using so many words, they have made it clear that someday, if the time comes, they want to be able to hire a live-in companion—that they foresee remaining independent of retirement homes and twenty-four-hour facilities. I drive them slowly through the old streets of Woodland, using the zeal of their commentary as my speedometer. When we pass the row of bungalows on Second Street, Dodie chirps her approval, and I stop the car.

The three of us take our time inside the sweet bungalow. It is airy and clean, and the potted plants settled in corners and on bookshelves catch Dodie's eye. Frank spends some time in the laundry room, which has a wall of closed cupboards that, Dodie tells me, would hold his tools and what not. She opens the cupboards in the kitchen and rests her hands against the sink counter.

"Are you tired, Dodie? Let's sit down." I pull out a wicker-seated chair from the kitchen table. In danger of overextending my realtor's rights, I take a clean glass from the cupboard above the dishwasher and fill it with bottled water from the fridge.

"It's more important that it's right for him," Dodie whispers to me after she sips her water. "It's Frank takes care of most things, these days."

"You each look so well," I say, wanting it to be both of them taking care, wanting to hear Dodie's refrain of concern for Frank's welfare the way I remembered it from my childhood.

"We sit a lot," she confessed. "You get up like we are—I am eighty-two, Dolores—and you spend a lot of time sitting."

"You have each other," I prod her. "You have sixty years of history together—"

"Yes we do. Yes we do. And that's something, isn't it?"

We hear Frank climbing the steps up the back porch, the creak of the screen door into the laundry room. He walks across the kitchen and puts both hands on Dodie's shoulders.

"What do you say, Mother? Think this will do us for thirty more years?"

Dodie laughs. "At least that, Frank."

I streamline the initiation of the escrow process as much as I can and promise Dodie and Frank that I'll be in touch with them as soon as the seller responds. It's not such a dreary idea, I think to myself as Frank pulls the Falcon carefully out from the curb, this growing old with a soul mate.

Back at the apartment, when Milton rubs against my legs demanding his attention, I think that Dodie and Frank may be the luckiest couple on my research roster. They've made it to a stage when simply sitting together at a table, with or without words, gives such satisfaction. I find it hard to imagine that Henry Talmouth and Ellen will ever reach that kind of matched ease. Daddy and my mother never had the chance. I am ashamed to see, with a sudden utter clarity, that whatever it is that Phil and Tammy Walters have today could in thirty years easily evolve into what Frank and Dodie Murphy have shown me.

I pick Milton up and whisper into his ear, "I hope that I'm that lucky."

CHAPTER SIX

Wild nights — wild nights!

Wild Nights—Wild Nights!
Were I with thee
Wild Nights should be
Our luxury!

Futile—the Winds—
To a Heart in port—
Done with the Compass—
Done with the Chart!

Rowing in Eden—
Ah, the Sea!
Might I but moor—Tonight—
In Thee!

EMILY DICKINSON 1861

A BRISK DELTA breeze is blowing by the time Rick Day and I have cleaned up after a day of sanding and scraping. I open every window in the house and watch the sawdust particles stirred by the moving air. The oak floors on the first story are now dulled by the circular sander, but next week after we've coated them with a satin sealer, they will glow as they must have in the 1800s. The floors have been the final chore of the resurrection of the Leland House; when the sealant sets, I will have to start thinking about bookshelves and furniture and my upcoming semester at Davis Law. For the past six weeks, I have lived refreshingly and completely in the immediate mechanical questions of the moment: deciding which sanding belt is demanded by which wood surface, whether to re-frame the upstairs windows or to totally replace each unit, how much the refashioned kitchen should rely on the technical wonders of microwave, dishwasher, trash compactor. In some suitable therapeutic process, I have reworked myself from the ground up, too, so that from day to day I feel as if I am meeting myself anew.

I finish a bottle of mineral water and set it on the kitchen counter, glad that I chose pine butcher block over tile. Outside the kitchen window, a potato vine trails its starlike white blossoms against the screen, the perfect yellow pistils a bright surprise. I was lucky to inherit it, Trevor Tuskes told me yesterday on one of his abrupt stopovers. The vines grow slowly, and to find one espaliered across a whole wall is a rarity. Rather than cut it back, I lay the entire vine against the ground when the painters worked up the kitchen side of the house. Then I cut strips of redwood lattice and rehung the vines on the layered diamond lattice pattern, up against the wall once again. The blooms slowed for a couple of weeks, but even Trevor has certified the plant's health.

I walk across the kitchen and into the front room, the parlor. The dark wainscoting is marbled by the sunlight sifting through the trees on Tryon Street. A flat, square box is leaning against the mantel—the beveled glass panes I ordered for the front door—and I shift the box into a safer position in the corner of the room. I'll finally get to replacing the glass, I tell myself. I shuffle through a stack of papers on my impromptu desk—the packing box the refrigerator arrived in—and find my calendar. Attached to it is a list of tasks I'd written up at the beginning of June. I sit down in a wooden rocker from my father's study, one of the few pieces of furniture I brought back from New York, and begin to line through the items I've accomplished. I've replaced the mailbox standing at the front gate, cleaned out the shed that sits behind the garage, ordered the glass panes for the front door, scheduled the required physical for the Foundation's health plan, picked out a corner office in King Hall, serviced the Jeep, and bought new spigots for the outside water lines. What I haven't done yet is decide whether to gut the plumbing in the bathroom upstairs or continue to live with the finicky squabbling that goes on between the running of shower water and the flushing of the toilet. And I need to find a suitable collection of pieces for the front room. But this will take time, I think, and wonder if Dolores knows anything about antiques.

A rush of images comes to mind when I think her name: Dolores turning to let Zoey button up her blouse; Dolores with her bare feet resting carelessly on her cluttered desk; Dolores wearing a Mexican wedding dress whirling between two cowboys at the Dance Palace; Dolores calling out Emily Dickinson's lines in the still summer dark; Dolores seated, Jorge's brown face pressed against her tousled blonde hair. What does it mean, I wonder, when a guy far too old to be foolishly falling in love feels himself so? Yesterday, in Woodland Drugs buying aspirin for a headache brought on by too much sun while setting posts for the back fence, I bought condoms, too. Not much room left for presumption of innocence, I tell myself. Clair Mariani would have a field day with this. I laugh out loud and check my watch. It's time to shower, if I can get the water pressure to agree, and to dress for my date in the first officially laundered shirt I've worn in over eight weeks.

At seven prompt, across town, Dolores opens the door. She's still wrapped in a blue robe, but she eyes me from the tip of my boots to the top of my hair.

"Pretty nice," she smiles at me. "I'll be a couple of minutes."

I call to her from the tiny kitchen, where Milton stands guard on the counter, switching his tail. "What's coming up in these peat pots?"

"More anemones. Trevor gave some to me a while ago, back when I was the master gardener at the Leland House. He intended those to go in the front, where the bricks make those oval beds? But these are for alongside the back walks. My housewarming. I'm going to plant them for you. They need to go in soon—can bulbs get root bound?"

After moving Milton from the counter to the kitchen table, I check the base of the nearest pot. "These little thready things coming out from the bottom roots?" I call back.

Dolores is beside me, taking the pot from my hands. "You know what they are, Mr. All-American know-it-all," she teases.

I turn to her and brush the hair back from her face.

"What do you see?" she asks.

"A master gardener I like so much it startles me," I tell her after a moment of silence, brushing her cheek where my fingers have left a trace of soil from the anemones.

Milton thumps onto the floor, and we pull apart.

"Sort of possessive, isn't he?" says Dolores.

"I can handle Milton," I joke with her. "Let's get out of here."

Out on the freeway, above the hum of the Jeep, I describe my campus office to Dolores. It's larger than I expected, with a view of the university greens from a window centered in the wall against which I'll put my desk. She asks me what kind of a professor I will be.

"Inflexible," I jest, and then go on. "The teachers I remember best—the ones I really learned from—they carried a quickness into class, in lectures and discussion, an alertness that kept us on our toes. It wasn't so much a matter of style as of substance, a kind of innate intelligence that engaged us and drew out our best. That's what I'd like to be, what I'll try for anyway."

"No *Paper Chase* intimidation?" she questions, half-serious.

"What's it prove? At any level, in any discourse, what's the point? If the point is victory by sheer bullying, which I have to say sometimes *is* the goal in the courtroom, then okay, yeah, intimidate. But if the point is consensus or the exercise of the intellect in order to solve a problem, then the exchange has to assume that both parties bring something of value to the discussion."

I grin, sheepish. "Sorry—I've been reading myself to sleep with pedagogical treatises on the Socratic method."

"Don't stop—I'm fascinated," Dolores prompts me. "It may seem a stretch, but some of what you're saying reminds me of what happens when you sell a house. You have to reserve judgment when you're defining the goal—what the buyers want? And there's always an incredible temptation to say, 'Now wait, I know exactly—even better than you—what you need . . .' Of course if you do that, then the sale never happens. Keep going!"

So I do, for the next ten miles into the city. Dolores stops me every now and then with keen questions that raise my enthusiasm for my subject. She reminds me of how changed my standpoint on the law will be in the life I have adopted. Yet it's not only law that revives itself for me now. The woman sitting beside me—the physical memory of her heart beating against mine in the welcome compulsory embrace of a western melody—recalls to life an atrophied longing, an ironic deficiency that tells me I am still, at forty-one, entirely capable of feeling needy.

On the streets of Old Sacramento we tarry on the wooden sidewalks, poking into the gimcrack shops and yogurt parlors and souvenir dens. In front of a glass door whose black letters read ALTMAN'S ANTIQUES AND COLLECTIBLES, I take Dolores's hand and pull her to my side.

"We've got ten minutes until our reservations. Will you come in with me to look at this stuff? I'm living in a house with virtually nothing to sit on."

Dolores pushes through the door ahead of me into the cool cave of the antique shop. The heavy scent of Old English furniture polish thickens the air. Dolores stops in front of a massive mahogany buffet.

"Did I mention my old friends Dodie and Frank Murphy?" she asks, stroking the mahogany's rounded edges. "They lived next door to us when I was growing up. Dodie had something like this in her dining room—on Easter Sunday she'd call me in and tell me to look for surprises. I would find dozens of these silver-wrapped chocolate eggs in drawers, tucked beneath her napkins and table linens."

She pauses. "But I think this is a little heavy for your house." She fingers the tag and murmurs, "And you're out of your mind to buy antiques in this tourist ghetto."

I nod my head at the proprietor, who has stepped from the beaded doorway to the back room at the sound of our voices. I take Dolores by the elbow.

"Just looking tonight, thanks," I tell him, and steer Dolores around a claw-footed bathtub to the door.

On the sidewalk again, stepping briskly around a loitering family of four, each of them dripping ice cream from gigantic cones, I ask her to tell me more about the Murphys.

"I showed them a house this morning on Second Street, a clean little bungalow—they need to get out from under so much maintenance. They're both in their eighties, but as bright and content as you could ask."

We stop in the foyer of the Sacramento River Delta Inn.

"I found myself envying them, so many years to look back on with fondness, years ahead still to sit together in silence. They seemed . . . so rich to me. It made me think."

She stops when the hostess, a red-haired woman with enormous silver loops in her ears who puts me in mind of Rick's girlfriend, Stacy, leads us to a shadowed table in the corner of the restaurant. Heavy exposed beams crisscross the ceiling of the dining room and dangle reproductions of gas lanterns, beneath whose sultry light we sit and smile at each other.

Dolores looks down at her table setting, then meets my eyes.

"It's you," she says softly. "I've lived forty years without having obsessive thoughts, and now I can't stop thinking them. It's you."

I put my hand on hers, press it against the blue linen of the tablecloth in what I know is a corny gesture but the right thing for me to do.

"You're not alone. You make me feel like a sixteen-year-old kid."

She locks eyes with me. "What you make *me* feel, Austin, is like nothing I recognize. I worry it's too good to be true."

"Pinch me," I say. "Or I'll pinch you, whatever you want. We're both real. We're lucky. It's real, Dolores."

Through the salad and the salmon and a lively disagreement about the relative merits of lecture versus guided discussion (how can one pretend to lecture to an audience that doesn't yet have the background to grasp the concepts, Dolores argues: it's contradictory), through the coffee and the return to the car in the night air cluttered by the chuckles and footsteps of fellow diners, we are weighted with anticipation. Some cosmic design long-awaited and well deserved has placed us where we stand, on the brink of completion, like the ancient Greek philosopher's unfinished selves who are destined to remain incomplete until they stumble across their missing half.

I reach across the Jeep's seat and take Dolores's hand in mine, weaving our fingers together. We trace the highway back to Woodland in silence, to a destination we have charted in common, without speaking, without words. I pull down Tryon Street to the house, my house, and look at Dolores.

"I should have put the anemones in the car and brought them over," she says.

"There will be plenty of time for you to do that," I say. "I'll even let you plant them."

"Thanks," she says and slips out the door.

She brushes the back of her hand against the petals of the blue iris which twist against the pickets of the front fence. I break a bloom from one of the flowers and hold it against her temple.

"You've done the house just the way I would have done," she says, holding the iris to her hair and stepping to the porch.

"Wait till you see inside. It's clean now, just waiting for furniture and rugs and—"

"And you," Dolores says, pulling me to her to kiss me. "You've come home, Austin."

We stand on the porch, its cant corrected by basalt blocks Rick and I maneuvered into position beneath the floor joists, its peeling paint stripped and sanded and redone, its doweled railings recut and refitted. I hold Dolores against me and breathe in the scent of her hair—a pure, little girl smell—and feel her arms around my

65

neck and know that it's true, that I have come home, that the place where I stand and the person in my arms belong to me as surely as anything I've ever known or done or held. I am heady with the feeling, giddy with a kind of recklessness born of the certainty that I am safe in harbor, that I've found my way home.

Inside, Dolores demands to see everything. I show her the kitchen first, the white-painted cupboards, the sanded pine counters, the enlarged window framed by the potato vine blossoms. She flicks lights on and off, opens drawers, and runs the water in the sink. She disappears into the pantry, where I have fitted a wine rack and spice shelf and potato and onion bins.

She pokes her head around the pantry door.

"I take this as a singular sign of character, Austin. That you've kept this walk-in pantry. It has so many uses," she says.

She tugs me into the cool, earth-smelling darkness of the tiny room. The door latches behind me, and she is in my arms again, her hands in my hair, her lips on mine. She breaks from our kiss.

"When did you know?" she asks me.

"Know?"

"When did you know about us?"

I stroke her waist, lean my forehead against hers.

"I'm not sure."

"No love at first sight?" she teases.

"It was something at first sight . . . I didn't know how to label it . . ."

Her breasts press against me, and I lower my head to kiss the hollow above her collarbone.

I whisper against her, "It was seeing you dart around town, half-dressed. I knew then you were a woman of wanton ways—"

Dolores pushes me against the wine rack.

"I should have known," she says, mock indignant. "It's always reduced to sex, isn't it?"

I lift her and hold her against me.

"Always, always, always," I say, teasing her back, "but first, you need to help me with my interior decorating."

In the parlor, Dolores stands in front of the manteled fireplace. She swivels and studies each wall of the room.

"First, Mr. Barclay, you want a sofa that sits facing the fireplace. Not overly large, but maybe overstuffed? And you want two wingbacks, not matched, here and here." She points to the ends of the imagined sofa.

I slip a tape into my portable player as she furnishes the room with her voice.

"George Jones?" she asks sweetly. "He won't go with what I had in mind."

"Bruce Springsteen," I tell her, and sing with the tape,

" 'Well here she comes a-walkin'
All that heaven will allow—' "

Then Dolores is again in my arms, and we dance the bare floor of the Leland House parlor while Springsteen sings about filling this house with all the love that heaven will allow. She is in my arms as we climb the stairs. She is in my arms as I lower her to the mattress on the floor where my sleeping bag is crumpled. Suddenly she is no longer in my arms but sitting straight up beside me.

"Austin?" She traces my lips with her fingers. "We're too old and responsible to be reckless here . . ."

"We won't be reckless," I say, shrugging to my feet. "I'm fully prepared."

"I knew you would be," she says, lying back against the sleeping bag.

I pull my shirt off and splash water on my face. The plumbing in the bathroom rattles. Beneath the sink, behind an overlooked box of sheetrock nails, I find the condoms. Like a kid, I tell myself, and grin into the mirror at my reflection, my dark hair, longer than it's been in years, my browned arms.

"I can't be late, I got a date with all that heaven will allow," I sing, loud enough for Dolores to hear.

"You need to get a real bed," she says when I lie down beside her.

We lie side by side in the silence. Together, as if we'd been cued by the same unspoken line, we turn to each other.

All my adult life, through both the casual encounters and the dutiful attempts at serious engagements, I've questioned the myth of conjugal unity, the fusion of souls promised by the archetypal moment of shared sexual splendor. What I found was never what the movies and fiction and poetry set up. As a kid I imagined that untrained passion would materialize when Caitlin Lamb and I were married; as a young man engaged in a series of mismatched relationships, I told myself that sex without love couldn't be expected to ante up to the real thing. Although I've never been disappointed by the beds that I've made, for almost twenty years I have allowed myself to live with the diminution, the downsizing, of the literary ideal. When Dolores and I turn to each other on the unzipped down bag in my refinished Woodland house, when we trip across a threshold that neither of us expected, we enter entirely a world of perfect touch, a world that renders one from two. Discovered by desire so fierce that the friction of our skin freezes my breath, I am lost to language until Dolores cries out. We kiss. We breathe. We kiss again.

I cradle her against my chest, my knees drawn up and fitted into the bended crook of hers. She holds my arm across her waist and runs her fingers down my forearm to my fingers, which she outlines one by one, and then palms against her own hand.

"You have hands like Dr. Chalmers," she says, gently pulling the hairs on my fingers.

"Ouch," I say against her neck, and pull her around to face me.

Later, as we lie still once again, Dolores traces the sweat on my chest.

"I need to use the ladies'," she says. She stands, a pale, slender shadow of a woman, and steps to the bedroom door. From the bathroom I hear the creaky flush of the toilet, the running of water in the sink.

In a moment she is beside me again.

"Does the water ever stop?" she asks, nuzzling my chin.

"I'll get it. I wanted to lie here with you. Not move for a time."

The water gurgles on until we can't bear it and burst into laughter.

"My turn," I say, heading for the hall. In the bathroom, I lift the tank top and jiggle the floating ball, waiting for the water level to rise.

In the night, when the air cools and I rise to cover us with a comforter, I study Dolores's face against the pillow. She breathes through parted lips. For a moment the slightest smile lifts her features in sleep: a half-remembered joke tickling her unconscious.

"Sweet dreams," I say and nestle against her warm outline.

Off and on throughout the night, I wake to the consolation of the sleeping woman beside me. There has never been anyone whom I've wanted to love the way I do this woman, who fits into the missing piece of my heart the way she does, whose every gesture and lilt pleases me with its utter familiarity.

I have found the contentment I sought for years without knowing what it was that I was seeking. Predawn light filters through the bedroom windows. In the trees on Tryon Street, the birds call out, a rash chorus of messages from the early morning, a mass from the leaf-laden branches of the old elms. I curl against Dolores, pull the comforter up against our chins, and fall back to sleep.

CHAPTER SEVEN

Pain —*expands the time* —

Pain—expands the Time—
Ages coil within
The minute Circumference
Of a single Brain—

Pain contracts—the Time—
Occupied with Shot
Gamuts of Eternities
Are as they were not—

EMILY DICKINSON 1864

EVERYTHING I DO puts me in mind of Austin.

If I stroke Milton's white scar, I hear Austin saying, "There's a boy . . . show me your war wounds, Milts."

If I run a brush through my hair, I feel Austin's fingers in it, combing the curls with his strong hands.

If I put my hand to my cheek, I feel Austin's lips against my skin.

Sometimes I find myself standing and staring, mesmerized by the memory of our lovemaking, the crests of feeling our love has pulled into being, waves as metered and inevitable as the real waves pulled back from all the beaches of the world by the strength of the moon.

I daydream as I load clothes into the washer. When I think of how literally Austin has walked into my life and transformed me from head to toe, I wonder how I could have lived without him for all the years that I have, how I could have remembered how to breathe before I knew what breathing was for. The whirring of the washer's motor reminds me to shut the lid, but I am caught up in another reverie: it is ages and ages hence, and Austin and I sit together at an oak table in the kitchen of the Leland House. He is gray and I am gray, and we are seated in wordless communion. The vision is filled with peace. I laugh out loud when I think of how my imaginings contrast with the stereotyped flush of first love. Instead of sweaty sex-filled bedroom scenes I am envisioning an elderly couple sitting together in silence. This must be, I swear to myself, the delirious transport of middle-aged passion. This must be what true love is.

My Saturday chores beckon. I empty Milton's cat box and run a mop across the kitchen floor. When the apartment—in dire need of attention for weeks—is tidied and Milton is snoring on the clean coverlet of my properly made bed, I sit down at my desk and turn on the computer. I have promised myself that I would transcribe the children's poems and surprise them with a Xeroxed book of their work, and even their scrawled lines are granted special meaning by my intoxicated state. I type through Soria's three verses about her baby brother and Lupe's backward slant describing what she thinks about in church and find Jorge's poem. He's titled it "My Dolores":

> Dolores likes to make us things
> And teach us how a poem sounds
> Dolores never makes a frown
> Dolores makes me sing.

Not bad for a second-grader, I smile to myself. The rhyme scheme is deliberate—abba—and Jorge has left finger smudges across the lined primer paper. I feel like singing myself, and I hum while I finish the poems, center them neatly in a bold type, and print out a draft copy. I sing through my shower and while dressing, while folding clothes from the dryer and making a grocery list, something I hardly ever do. I will take the disk of poems down to the office and run them on the laser printer, and then run the whole book over to the Color Copy Shop to have it printed on a thick blue bond and spiral bound. And then I will shop carefully because I have told Austin that I will cook dinner in his newly equipped kitchen, the kitchen that figures so prominently in my fantasies of geriatric bliss. I open a can of tuna for Milton, even though it's too early for his supper, and give him one last pat after I gather up the papers from my desk. He turns his head but doesn't bother to open his eyes. Absolute devoted trust is what Milton has for me. Absolute devoted trust is where good relationships end up, I think, if people are anything like cats.

The phone rings as I am walking down the sidewalk to the Volvo. I stop, consider running back to the house, and then decide to let it ring. It's too hot to run, and that's what answering machines are for, I remind myself. I head to the office.

I have barely unlocked the realty door when the throbbing bell on Zoey's desk pierces the close silence of the office. I punch her line and answer with a breathless, halfway angry "Hello?"

"It's me." Austin's voice, but it's not right.

"I'm sorry—I was rushing to get the kids' book together—I don't usually take office calls on Saturday after—"

"Dolores, I'm in a fix here."

"Austin?"

"I've cut my hand, is what I've done—I don't think I can drive—"

"I'm coming. I'm on my way. Did you wrap it? Press, press! Hold it up. I'm coming."

I am sick to my stomach as the Volvo screeches around the turn onto Tryon Street. I fling open the door and run up the brick walk, push through the screened front door, and step over a cracked pane of glass.

"Austin?" My voice is hardly more than a whisper.

"In the kitchen."

I trail a path of blood across the shining oak floor to the kitchen door. For just one hysterical second I remember Hansel and Gretel, and I tell myself that it's just a cut, that people get cuts and live through them every day, all the time, all over California, all over the world. I look up. Austin is leaning over the kitchen sink, his right hand bound clumsily in a flowered yellow dish towel that is growing redder and redder even as I watch.

"You need to hold it up," I tell him and lift his elbow up to his chest. I rifle through two drawers before I find a clean dish towel, this one green-checked. I can do this, I tell myself, and I unwrap the bloodied towel from his hand.

It's an ugly ragged cut, extending from the center of Austin's palm across to the base of his thumb, and it won't stop bleeding. I press the clean towel hard against the wound.

"Bend your thumb over, to close it. Can you hold it for a minute?"

Austin nods. He looks pale.

"Where's the duct tape?" I try to joke. "I knew that extralarge roll would come in handy—"

"In the third drawer."

I make Austin sit down on the floor, and I cover his hand with a second towel that I swathe into place with long strips of the heavy tape.

I sit down beside him. "Ready to go? You need stitches, lots of them."

I brush his hair back from his face, pale even beneath his carpenter's tan.

He turns his lips against the hand I have on his shoulder.

"I love you," he says.

"I know," I answer him. "Let's get you stitched up."

Austin is paler still in the emergency room, where a stocky nurse leads us into a curtained cell. She makes him lie down on the crisp white sheet of the surgical bed while she pulls on a pair of rubbery gloves. I stand at his head, stroking his hair. His eyes are shut, and he looks, to me, to be very tired. I read her name card, TAMARA, while she unwraps Austin's hand. Austin tenses, and I look away when she swabs the cut with a soapy mixture.

"What happened here?" Tamara asks, feigning an interest that must be hard to muster at the end of a twelve-hour shift. I feel sorry for her, for the exhaustion that keeps her from knowing her patient as I do, how special he is, how irreplaceable. I bend down to kiss Austin's forehead.

He opens his eyes.

"Absolute foolishness. Breaking every rule in the *Boy Scout Handbook*. I forced a pane of glass."

Tamara dabs Austin's hand with a dry towel.

"I'd say you did a first-rate job of it. You've just missed severing the major flexor here—doctor will have to stitch up the muscle first, then the skin."

"No more hammering, almost," Austin says, and rolls his eyes back at me, a sign that I shouldn't worry anymore, that he wants me to know everything will be okay.

Tamara gives Austin two shots, and then the emergency room doctor is there, swiveling up to Austin's hand on a three-legged stool, stitching so fast he is done almost as soon as he started. He writes Austin two prescriptions, tells him to see his regular physician to have the external stitches checked in five days, and swivels out of the cell.

"He's had a long day," Tamara apologizes, helping Austin to his feet. "You steady now? Can your wife help you with the paperwork?"

"His wife can," I tell her and push Austin into a chair in the waiting room. I follow Tamara to the admissions desk, where she hands me a clipboard and a pen. Beside Austin, his head resting on my shoulder, I record his dictated answers to the questions on the hospital form. I fish his wallet from his back pocket to find his insurance card and hold the clipboard close to his left hand so he can scrawl a dubious signature.

"You look done in," I tell him as I rise to return the papers.

"I am. I am an exhausted, clumsy carpenter wanna-be who had no business breaking that glass—"

"No, you're not, never, ever." I kneel in front of him, his bandaged hand in mine. "You had one accident. One accident. You're not clumsy." I kiss his swaddled hand. "Not clumsy," I say again, and kiss his eyes, his cheeks, his lips.

"You're everything to me," I tell him, and I see by saying it I've made it true.

I drive slowly across town to take Austin home. The Leland House is almost completely renovated now, from the gracious flowering beds to the sparkle of the new glass in the second-story windows. The temperature shifts from the sidewalk to the garden, when the interlacing leafy boughs of the elms and birches canopy the cool dark loam. Even with its imbalanced corner tower and its dangerously coy and frivolous detail, the house seems to pledge another hundred years.

Austin takes my arm as we walk up the front porch steps.

"I'll clean it," I say when he grimaces at the shards of glass littering the entryway. "But first you ought to lie down."

Upstairs in Austin's bedroom I strip the sheets from his new bed, delivered as soon as the floors were dry. I find a set of clean linen in the hall closet and make up the bed.

"With hospital corners, since you're used to them," I tell him, looking for a smile. He gives me one, wan and weak, but at least a smile.

The bed open, Austin slides onto the sheets. I pull off his shoes.

"I'll be myself after some sleep."

"You are yourself now." I bend over him and kiss his temple. "Will you want dinner, the way we said?"

"For sure."

He is asleep before I reach the bedroom door, enervated by the headlong ebb of energy that trauma always leaves in its wake. I don't want him to worry—I still want to make this day good.

Austin's hand will heal, the glass will be replaced—I will have a glazier come out before he wakes—and we will still be in love with each other.

In the kitchen I start a kettle for coffee and sit down at the round oak table that Austin discovered at a yard sale on the east side of town. The day he showed it to me, sitting in the back shed, it looked dusty, almost charred, and half the wooden beading that ran around the lip was missing. Two days later, when I stopped after work to put down the anemones, the table was standing in the center of the kitchen, the beading faithfully replaced, the dark oak glistening. There is a flat iron burn mark under my hand—Austin said it was a bonus, this historical artifact from another era—which he hadn't even tried to sand out. Too deep, he told me, and besides, it belonged there, the reminder of someone else's hard work performed at this table. Look at the ribbing on the pedestal foot, he said kneeling, so boyish and proud that I had to throw my arms around him and halt his words with my kisses. He re-creates everything with his eager touch: the house, the garden, the table, even me. I wrap my arms around my chest to stop myself from shivering, from imagining a world without Austin.

The glazier will charge me double, but he promises to be out in a half hour to set the remaining panes. He thinks he has something—a piece of stained glass—that will fill in for the broken plate if I don't care that it doesn't match. I tell him that whatever he can do will make me happy, that I want the door finished. I sip my coffee and fill a bucket with soapy water while I wait for him. I scrub the kitchen counter, the sink, and the trail leading backward to the front door. By the time the glazier arrives, the accident scene is spotless. I don't offer him an explanation of what has happened, except that we just decided to get the darn door done. Crazy yuppies, he's probably thinking, throwing money away on a whim.

He shows me two choices that could stand in for the broken pane. One is patterned with an unreasonably colored bird—too garish, I tell him. The other is etched with a vine of some sort, maybe berries, and I think yes, this will do. In twenty minutes the panes are set, and I write a check and wave the glass man out of the house. Upstairs, I tiptoe to the door of Austin's room. He is still asleep. Even though it's warm, I pull the sheet up over his shoulders before I leave.

Four hours behind my original schedule, I return to the office and run prints of the children's poems. After dropping the laser copies off at the Copy Shop and choosing paper in Jorge's favorite blue, I park beneath a struggling olive tree in the lot at Podesta's, Woodland's gourmet grocery, where Zoey has told me with unabated scorn that if I really try I can spend forty dollars for a jar of mustard. I pull the crumpled paper list from my handbag. My handwriting—I can't believe it was only this morning that I scratched out this list for a lovers' feast!—recalls another season, a world away, a sphere where the possibility of pain beyond suffering was inconceivable. I want to will myself back in time six hours to the untainted anticipation of absolute, innocent rapture. I am being melodramatic, I tell myself, and stride into the store, defying Zoey and common sense as I purposefully buy the most expensive mushrooms, the best balsamic vinegar, a whole frond of dried tarragon.

The tarragon perfumes the kitchen when I crumble it into melted butter and chopped garlic.

"You *can* cook," a voice says from the staircase.

Austin walks into the kitchen on bare feet, his hair rumpled.

"How is it?" I ask, laying the wooden spoon against the stove top.

"Sore as heck . . . and I feel foolish." He lowers himself gingerly into a chair, resting his bandaged hand against the table top, covering the black outline of the flat iron.

I stand behind him, massaging the taut muscles in his shoulders. He catches my arms with his good hand.

"It smells great in here."

"Tarragon chicken, Greek salad, mushrooms, French bread," I breathe into Austin's ear. "And if you can, a glass of Sémillon?"

I barbecue the chicken on Austin's patio, a circle of slate beneath a redwood bower—Aunt Emmabelle's one contemporary bequest—that's covered with heavy wisteria vines. We have a second glass of the white wine. I turn the chicken and lift it onto our plates.

As I cut Austin's chicken, I ask, "Will you let the hired hands do whatever else is left now?"

He waits for me to sit and spread my napkin in my lap. He takes an awkward left-handed bite of the chicken.

"It's good, Dolores. So is the wine."

"That wasn't my question." I feel parental, grim.

"Okay, okay. There's hardly anything left . . . I can't do much one-handed, anyway—"

"I should say not. You're virtually helpless."

He winks at me. "Not helpless . . . not completely."

The meal I have made *is* good, and I decide to let myself relax. Intellectually, I know that vigilance won't forestall disaster, that disaster will come awaited or by surprise, but the man sitting across the table in the fading summer light is so precious to me that I need to breathe deep and let it go before I spoil the evening. It's my age, it's the wise skepticism of experience that commands these alarums signaling a distrust in happiness. Our forks chime against Austin's flowered china, china that could be a match to my mother's, finally unboxed after sitting through the summer on the floor of the parlor. I pass the butter, spoon extra mushrooms onto Austin's plate. I manage to let go of the illogical fear that I've felt all afternoon. I make myself manage.

The dishes are rinsed, the dishwasher running, the counters scrubbed when I ask Austin whether I should stay or go home.

"Don't go home," he says and pulls me to him. "You belong here tonight. Just as much as you ever did."

I hold his white-wrapped hand in mine.

"Since I belong here, I want to show you something."

I steer him to the entryway, where all four panes of the front door are alive with reflected light from the hallway.

"It's not beveled, but it's done," I say, cautious.

He touches the etched glass of the mismatched fourth pane with his fingertips.

"I like it. It's you, one hundred percent. An in-your-face refusal to comply. I like it."

"Better than plywood, anyway," I offer. "And the theme of this house is imbalance, as I'm sure you've noticed."

"Speaking of imbalance, I could call it a night. If you can."

"A day and a night," I say, taking Austin's untaped arm and draping it over my shoulder.

We climb the stairs together, arms laced. I pull his shirt over his shoulders for him, watch him walk out of the bedroom, and listen to the finicky pipes chortling in the bathroom.

"You may be on water duty tonight," he says as he nudges into bed beside me.

"It's a deal," I say and pull his dark head against my breast.

"Thank you, Dolores. For today . . . and for finding me."

"You found me, sweetheart. You found me."

I feel his breathing soften and slow until I know he is sleeping.

Whatever the popular romantics may say to the contrary, whatever *Cosmo* and *Esquire* may pronounce, when I hold this man safe and chaste against my heart, I feel an intimacy that I am sure the most wild and abandoned sex has never inspired. With my fingertips, I follow the outline of his brow, his cheekbone, his chin. I press my lips against his hair and breathe in the smell of him. His good hand curls around mine when I stroke his palm. We are linked hand to hand, heart to heart, breath to breath. I have never been this close to anyone, not Daddy, not Todd, not Henry Talmouth. It frightens me, this demanding intimacy, not because I am losing myself in it but because I am finding myself, because it is making me whole as I have never been. Everything about the man in my arms soothes me: even his fastidious idiosyncrasies which clash with my haphazard sloppiness and his gentle assessments of what I would label the most idiotic behaviors—even these sit right with me so that I feel like the scale in my soul is balanced for the first time in my life.

I shift myself down against the pillows and roll Austin's weight so he lies on his left side. I nestle against him and wrap my arm around his bandaged hand, lifting it so it rests on the bedcovers. A stray breeze lifts the curtain at the window of the bedroom window and touches our faces. We lie together like spoons.

In sickness and in health, I say to myself, and fall asleep.

CHAPTER EIGHT

It's easy to invent a life——

⬥

It's easy to invent a Life—
God does it—every Day—
Creation—but the Gambol
Of His Authority—

It's easy to efface it—
The thrifty Deity
Could scarce afford Eternity
To Spontaneity—

The Perished Patterns murmur—
But His Perturbless Plan
Proceed—inserting Here—a Sun
There—leaving out a Man—

EMILY DICKINSON 1863

I HAVE BEEN unpacking boxes for two days. The floor-to-ceiling pine shelves that Rick Day put up for me on the east wall of the parlor are almost filled; the cardboard boxes scattered around my feet nearly empty. Everything I own, everything I had shipped out from New York, has found its way into cupboards and closets, shelves and drawers. I did much of the arranging one-handed, but now the lighter bandage around my stitched hand allows more movement, and this morning I will finish the books and be done. Be done except for the one remaining housewarming task—to find the sofa and wingbacks that will complete this room. At the bottom of the last packing box, I find a manila envelope marked in Lupe's hand: "Mr. Austin—mirror." I slide my hand inside the oversize envelope and pull from it my hiking picture, the one that I kept for years in the mirror on the oak dresser from my childhood bedroom. The dresser is upstairs filled with clothes, but I think that I'll find a frame to protect the worn photograph and let it sit on the shelves here, among the books.

When I have flattened the boxes and toted them out back to the recycle bin and centered the Indian carpet on the swept parlor floor, I ease myself into the rocker and lean my head against the chair back, contemplating the semester, which starts next week. I am lucky to share a first-rate secretary and a benevolent dean. The first-rate secretary, Annie Martin, has set up the computer in my office in King Hall and arranged the few law books I inherited from my predecessor on the bookshelves rendered obsolete by electronic access to the law library. Yesterday when I drove into campus, I found her perched atop a three-step ladder, dusting the farthest reaches of the highest shelf. She climbed down the ladder, extended her hand, and spent the next two hours showing me the ins and outs of local E-mail and the computerized class roster and grading system. The benevolent dean, John Decker, has given me an ideal academic schedule, which has me teaching mornings and holding office hours in the early afternoon. Doing carpentry on the house provided the perfect transition from New York to California living, but I am thankful it's done, that the Leland House is now my home and the tidy notes for my first week's lectures are sitting completed on the desk in my study.

My eyes fall on a vase of purple gladiolas. Dolores spied them blooming in the side yard and argued with me whether to cut them or let them bloom untouched. You'll see them inside, she debated convincingly against my naturalist protests, and left the kitchen with clippers in hand. They stood in a wine carafe until yesterday, when she brought over the cut glass vase. One of the few things she'd saved from her mother's kitchen, she told me, running water over the glad stems as she snipped them to fit in the vase. I told her she was growing domestic. She splashed me, two-handed, before turning back to the flowers and posing them artfully in the cut glass. I told her that I could see I'd exhausted the sympathy deserved by invalids, and she rolled her eyes at me. She was a businesswoman, not a nurse, she reminded me over her shoulder.

She is businesswoman, nurse, teacher, poet, comedienne, my lover. I say these words over and over to myself—my lover—and recall her hands stroking my hair as I lay in the hospital bed vaguely aware of the surgical thread tugging skin and muscle together. She has a side to her I've only detected in vignettes with Jorge, a capacity for carekeeping without belittling, for taking care without taking. More than this, I suspect she would allow herself to be cared for, if the need arose, despite the strong successful single woman demeanor at which she likes to playact. Yet she can be absolutely calculating and unsentimental, too, as she was when she outlined the relative joys to be had from living flowers rarely viewed versus cut flowers in constant sight.

The gladiolas remind me that I need to cement our plans for the upcoming Nevada City antique hunt and my last weekend as an unemployed man, so I rise from the rocker and head for the kitchen to phone the realty.

Zoey picks up. After making me promise to give her a tour of the renovated house, she turns me over to Dolores.

"Hello there." Dolores uses her office voice.

"About the weekend—the antique hunt? Are we on?"

"I'll have to check my social calendar—"

"I thought *I* was your social calendar."

"Then we must be on," she banters.

"For real, now," I say. "I'll make Saturday reservations at a bed and breakfast on Broad Street—fair enough? We'll leave early and meander our way up the mountain?"

"How early?"

"If it's too early I'll come get you out of bed."

She laughs at this and tells me yes, the weekend is on.

I remember Nevada City as my father's lunch stop on the return from our backpacking trips, but I don't expect it will be unchanged. The bed and breakfast I pick is the Sargent House on the far end of Broad Street. The proprietress tells me it was built in 1856 by civic leader and former U.S. Senator Aaron A. Sargent. She doesn't advise me to buy from any of the antique dealers close to town but assures me that I'll find plenty of samples in her rooms. To give me ideas, she says, friendly.

I am stepping off the porch on my way to campus when I hear the phone ring. I'll be back in three hours, I tell myself; I will answer it then. As I set a box of papers into the back of the Jeep, the faint ringing ceases.

Even though it's lunch hour when I climb the stairs to my office in King Hall, Annie is working at her computer screen, a half-eaten tuna sandwich sitting on a napkin beside a carton of chocolate milk. I'll talk to her when she's done, I tell her when I poke my head inside her door. The rest of the building is silent, a hollow vessel waiting to be filled with footsteps, slamming doors, the echoes of student conversation.

My office is light, the desk uncluttered. On the screen of my computer are three stick-up notes. The first, pink, is dated yesterday, 11:45. In Annie's hand it reads "Call Dr. Hindari re retesting." I puzzle over that and pull the second, blue, from the screen: "Hello Professor Barclay. I'm enrolled in your 10:30 Contracts section. I have to be out of town on Monday for inescapable family duties, but please note I'll be back Tuesday. Jason Loman." Cheeky kid already, I think, musing over the "inescapable," not sure whether or not I ought to be pleased that he had the foresight to excuse himself from class before his absence. The third, pink again, is a repeat of the first, dated this morning, about the time I left Woodland to drive in to campus: "Call Dr. Hindari," it says, Annie's loopy letters filling the square of colored paper.

I flip on the computer and listen to its warm-up whine. In the neat pile of paperwork centered on my desk, I find the list of health plan doctors and copy down Hindari's number. I dial and count the rings: three, four, five.

"Doctor's office. Carlene speaking."

"Carlene? I'm a new patient of Dr. Hindari's, Austin Barclay. I had a physical two weeks ago. *B-A-R-C-L-A-Y*. I have a message here to call—"

"Yes, the doctor wanted to speak to you himself, but he's in surgery now. Will you call back at about three-thirty?"

I tell her yes, wonder briefly about the purpose of Hindari's calls, and forget him completely when Annie walks through the door with a printout of the registration rosters.

"You want to show me how to enter an excused absence, first day of class?" I ask her.

We spend the next two hours exploring electronic attendance systems, faculty rotation lists, the meeting maker calendar, and advisory duties. My crash course in academic bookkeeping almost over, I thank Annie and tell her I'll see her first thing Monday morning, come hell or high water.

"On day one, you'll be wishing for high water," she laughs to me and steps back to her office.

The pink notes, which I have stuck to the corner of my desk, catch my eye as I stand to leave. I try Dr. Hindari's office one more time. A woman's voice, not Carlene's this try, tells me the doctor is in conference, asks is there a number where I can be reached. I remind her she has my home phone in her files, vow I'll call again, and hang up. At home in Woodland, I erase two more of Carlene's messages from the answering tape and consider calling the clinic one last time. Briefly it occurs to me that the hospital emergency room must have forwarded papers concerning the treatment for my hand, that the good doctor wants an update on the stitches; then I put the matter aside. It is nearly five-thirty, so I recradle the phone and figure I'll try again Monday from my office before classes.

On Saturday morning, I take time to swing by Eddie's to pick up the *New York Times* from the box, but I am at Dolores's apartment by seven-thirty. I knock and wait, knock again. I am just contemplating the penalties for breaking and entering when the door swings open and Dolores peeks around it, her hair a riot of curls, Garfield socks on her feet.

"I thought you'd let me sleep in," she complains in a voice softened by sleep, nudging Milton aside with her orange-striped foot.

"*I* thought we'd get an early start."

"What's the rush? Come back to bed with me. We have all the time in the world." She tugs me into her bedroom and pushes me onto the disheveled mound of blankets and sheets that still holds the warmth of her sleeping form.

"You're a hard one to rouse," I say to her when she's cuddled against me.

"We'll see who's hard to rouse," she smiles, unbuttoning my shirt.

When we awake at, as Dolores calls it, the more respectable hour of ten, I study her puttering around the kitchen, making coffee, feeding Milton, pushing a lock of her tangled hair off her forehead. She is still wearing a faded Cal football jersey and the surprising orange socks. How completely without guile she is, I wonder, as I watch her straighten the paper ("The *Times* delivered! An unthinkable luxury in Woodland!"). She settles Milton into her lap and sips at her coffee. Later, on Highway 80 above Auburn, I turn to watch her as she sits, her slender legs drawn up so her bare feet are against the dashboard, her face turned to catch the wind. I reach my taped hand over to rest in her lap.

"So you spent time up here with your dad?" she asks, turning to me and sliding her sunglasses up to the bridge of her nose.

"Lots of time. He was a biochemist, in the lab most of his working life, and he loved these mountains. His dad, my grandfather, brought his family up here throughout the thirties, before the advent of the superhighways. Dad used to tell me that the lab was pure science, but the mountains were pure poetry."

Dolores lies back against the seat.

"How about yours?" I ask. "You all were campers, too, weren't you?"

She laughs.

"My father had this Rambler station wagon when Todd and I were small. He used to let us pack it ourselves—we'd have to live with our choices, he'd say—and we'd fill it with blankets and toys and books and canned spaghetti and then tell him, okay, Daddy, we're ready. Then we'd head up-country until Daddy would find some hike that looked good, and we'd be off for the day. At night we'd come back to the Rambler, our base camp, we called it, and eat whatever we'd brought and sleep in the car with the seats folded down."

She pauses, looks out the window at the oaks and pines flashing by.

"When he let us make those choices? He knew *he* would have to live with them, too."

I stroke her thigh.

"When we got older, it was real backpacks and sixty-dollar boots and down bags and then, of course, we didn't want to go to the mountains with our chaperone father anymore." She laughs. "Especially in a Rambler, for God's sake."

As I listen to Dolores tell stories about her family, I think about how we come to know someone, how hearing a person reinvent her past offers as much definition of who she is now as does the cut of her hair or the title on her business card. Or the fact that she wears Garfield socks to bed.

"Your turn," she says, her eyes filled with laughter. "All about the high school sweetheart. Spill the beans."

Or that she asks impertinent questions.

"She was the quietest girl in my graduating class. So quiet, so sweet, that you could imagine she was thinking or feeling whatever you wanted her to be thinking or feeling—my pitfall—and throughout high school I always thought I would marry her."

"And live happily every after?"

"Then I would have said yes, but now I can see pretty clearly that happily ever after wouldn't have ever come—or come too soon, depending on how you look at it . . . but . . ."

"But?"

"Even when you know that something is foolish, or inappropriate, or just mistaken, there's a residue . . . a distillation of emotion that doesn't wash away . . . you can look at the specific details of, say, a relationship and realize sure, this was a loser from the get-go, but there's a feeling left, some kind of romantic expectation that gets recycled and finds its way into what you want for the present—"

"Hah! So I'm not the only one guilty of downsizing my expectations."

"I think you've just defined growing up."

"Have I? Either growing up or Henry Talmouth," Dolores says flatly.

"What?"

"You think I'm a nice person, but I'm not . . . I had an affair with a married man . . . a very upscale married man."

"I still think you're a nice person."

She looks at me; she can't resist: "I used to smoke."

"Ooooh, bad girl." I laugh at her.

"I lied about my experience when I got my first job."

"You'll have to do better than that."

"I . . . rarely clean my apartment."

"You feed your cat."

"I pick on Zoey."

"Zoey picks on you . . . give up?"

"I quit when I can't win."

This time I can't resist: "You're supposed to quit when you're ahead."

Dolores moans and slaps my shoulder. "I set myself up."

"You sure did."

The Sargent House is flashy—flashier than my tastes approve, but it's charming and authentic nonetheless. The window of our suite looks out on a tailored lawn which runs downhill to Deer Creek, moving slow and shallow in the early autumn California drought. The ribboned details of the hand-quilted cover on the brass bed are accented by a painted border running along walls just beneath the twelve-foot ceiling. Now that's too tacky, Dolores giggles, so loudly that I cup my bandaged hand over her mouth and force her to the bed, which only makes her laugh harder.

"I know who would love this decor," she grins at me when I lift my hand.

"I'm not going to encourage you," I say in admonition.

"You're just like Zoey," she says. Then quickly, as I pretend to muzzle her, "Okay, okay—I'll be nice. I promise. I'll be nice."

"I told you . . . you are nice," I say, kissing her until she's quiet.

"Do you want to do it *again?*" she asks, her hands inside my shirt.

"Of course I do," I say. "That's why I brought you here."

We do make love again, the second time in six hours in the early afternoon mountain light, as if we are at once teenagers and a couple long-married, touch telling us more about each other than a conversation would ever yield, yet our desire as much concerned with the secret places of the soul as with the private transports of the body. It is as if Dolores becomes more Dolores with every conversation, every act of love, and I, by transposition, become more myself.

It is Dolores who rises and insists that we hit the streets. We can at least be somewhat athletic decadents, she tells me on her way into the bathroom. We have, after all, come to the mountains on a mission.

The mission takes us up and down Nevada City's streets. We easily tire of the artsy stores that clutter the tourist walkways and soon find ourselves well off the beaten path, studying the tended miniature gardens of the real homes, not postcard glamorous and dolled up with San Francisco colors, but lived in and tempting: a tire swing hanging from an oak tree in this yard, three black and white kittens spilling from an abandoned dresser drawer under the rose bush in that one. Dolores discovers the faded velvet love seat covered by yellowed newspapers pinned down by three pieces of split cedar, its cushions disgorging stuffing across the worn blue paint of the unremarkable house's small porch.

"There you go," she says, grabbing my arm. "Check out that wooden scroll work. You have an upholsterer restuff and recover it—it will be perfect!"

"It's somebody's home," I correct her. "This isn't a shop, there aren't any for sale signs hanging on it."

"Silly! You knock on the door and make an offer. The worst thing they can say is 'no.'"

"But somebody lives there . . . we'd be invading their privacy."

"What you don't know about sales." She heaves an exaggerated sigh.

Before I can stop her, she is walking down the curbside steps and knocking on the front door. A lace curtain pulls aside from the single window facing the porch. Moments later, the door opens. An immensely pregnant girl, her lank brown hair falling around her face, listens to Dolores, who speaks quickly, waving her hands at the sofa.

"I don't know what my husband would want . . . that doesn't sound like very much," I hear the girl say, her voice slow. A television in the room behind her fills the air with disingenuous laughter.

"We could go fifty," Dolores compromises. "But no higher."

"We'll go one fifty," I say, taking the stairs two at a time, reaching for my wallet as I stomp onto the porch. "Will your husband agree to that?"

"But—" Dolores stammers.

"Thank you," I say firmly to the girl, who has already extended her hand for the neatly folded bills I place into it.

"I think he will," she says. "I think he will." The door closes, muting the moronic voices from the television.

"Austin!" Dolores says, aghast. "You could have had it for fifty! I could have got it for fifty!"

"I can pay more," I say. "They obviously need it, a kid on the way—it wasn't for sale to begin with."

"That's the point! It wasn't for sale—nobody else has offered them a penny for it—it's pure profit to them!"

I take Dolores by the shoulders and pull her close. "Are we having a difference in moral judgment here?"

"Not a moral difference, a practical one."

"The businesswoman speaking?"

"The realist speaking. If the range of possibilities—"

"Stop," I say, holding my fingertips to her mouth. "The girl is happy, we're happy. Let's stop this now."

For a moment she looks as if she wants to say one thing more, to have the last word. Then she purses her lips, turns on her heel, and calls to me as she climbs the steps to the sidewalk, "I know a good upholsterer in Woodland—he's on the corner of Main and Fifth."

After dinner in the National Hotel, after a moonlit walk up Tribulation Trail, after Dolores is asleep beside me, her bare arms holding the trendy comforter against her breast, I remember her determined march to the door of the little house, her resolute proposal to the haggard mother-to-be. Rather than make her less lovable, this hard edge she has shown amplifies her goodness, elevating its value by contrast. Clair Mariani comes to mind, her decisive and sometimes vicious diatribes, and I begin to understand how Jack might be able to love her. I fall to sleep congratulating myself for discovering that when we love, we love whole people, not discrete attributes, and resolve that the sofa will be recovered in dark blue. And that I will ask Dolores to move in with me.

Early Monday morning, when I am finishing my coffee in the Leland House's bright kitchen, I look up the name of the upholstery shop Dolores mentioned and jot down its number on my calendar. Attached to the pink slips of Annie's messages, I read the reminder to myself that I've printed in square letters over Annie's sweeping strokes: call Dr. Hindari first thing Monday. As soon as I walk into my office, I pick up the phone and dial the clinic. Carlene tells me the doctor is in. Waiting for him, I draw circles on the pink message paper. By the time Hindari reaches the phone, I have obliterated every word of the original message.

"Hello, Mr. Barclay. I was going to have Carlene try you again this morning," he says, his accent Indian, gracious.

"You're a hard man to reach," I say.

"Single physician clinic . . . the curse of Hippocrates." He laughs, a tired cough. "But you've reached me now, which is good, because we need to rerun some blood tests—the lab people are understaffed, as well, and they seem to have botched this panel."

"And?"

"You're not to worry . . . we just need to draw more blood."

"Great . . . another day of bloodletting in Davis." I reach behind the computer and press the on button, lulled by the intonations of Dr. Hindari's deep voice.

"Yes—it won't take up much of your time . . . but as soon as possible? To complete the required paperwork for the physical, if you could this afternoon—"

"I'll come by in the late afternoon. Will that work?"

"Sure. Carlene will have the forms out—we'll have you in and out and get those tests rerun."

"Fair enough. Thank you, doctor."

The first day of classes moves past in a whirlwind, and I am caught up in the September thrill of new faces, new subjects, new intellectual territory. My introductory lectures go well, even though I am finding my way as I speak. Not a courtroom, I have had to remind myself throughout the day, not a courtroom but a conference of sorts. I am so engrossed in reviewing my encounters with students and colleagues that I nearly forget my appointment at Hindari's clinic.

It is almost five when I pull into the parking slot directly in front of the squat stucco building housing the Davis Medical Corporation. Carlene looks up from her desk as I step into the reception area.

"Oh, Mr. Barclay, you're here. Doctor Hindari wanted to see

you himself. Have a seat for just a sec." She disappears behind a frosted glass door.

It is only a moment before the door reopens and Dr. Hindari beckons me into the lab room. He is a portly man, heavy featured but gentle. He gestures me into a yellow plastic chair with an arm-rest on the left side.

He talks as he snaps on a pair of rubber gloves. "As long as you are here, why don't I look at that hand?" he suggests.

"I'd like to get rid of the taping." I say, stretching out my left arm on the armrest, clumsily rolling up my shirt sleeve with my bandaged hand.

He takes the blood, three vials of it, while I watch. The process reminds me of my father, his careful measurements, his meticulous movements within the pure science of his laboratory. Dr. Hindari caps the third vial, pens what appears to be an illegible note on the adhesive label—no wonder the lab makes mistakes, I think to my-self—and pulls my sleeve down. He surprises me by buttoning the cuff of my shirt and patting my wrist before speaking.

"What did you do with the hand, then?" He unwraps the gauze from my right hand and pokes and presses at the seamed line of healing flesh.

I tell him about the house, the door glass, the single mis-matched etched pane, which will always denote my carelessness but which seems now to belong to the character of the Leland House.

He has finished retaping my hand with a narrow strip when I finish my recital. I flex my fingers.

"A world of difference," I tell him.

"It's healing well," he says, scratching more impossible notes on his chart. He stands, slides the chart into a shelf, strips the rub-ber gloves, and runs water to scrub his hands. His back to me, he speaks again. "It may be ten days—we'll call—I'll call as soon as the results come back."

"So I shouldn't worry?" I am joking with him, but he doesn't seem to realize.

"No, no worry now. Till we see you, then." He doesn't turn to face me as I say good-bye. It takes me several seconds of watching his back, his shoulders working as he rinses his hands again and again, to register that I've been dismissed. Carlene is nowhere to be seen when I walk through the reception room.

Funny guy, Dr. Hindari, I say to myself as I climb into the Jeep and head for home.

CHAPTER NINE

A house upon the height —

A House upon the Height—
That Wagon never reached—
No Dead, were ever carried down—
No Peddler's Cart—approached—

Whose Chimney never smoked—
Whose Windows—Night and Morn—
Caught Sunrise first—and Sunset—last—
Then—held an Empty Pane—

Whose fate—Conjecture knew—
No other neighbor—did—
And what it was—we never lisped—
Because He—never told—

EMILY DICKINSON 1862

I SETTLE THE potted tea rose onto the floor of the Volvo's back-seat, bracing the base with a pair of my old tennis shoes, interrupted en route to the Goodwill, so it won't tip when I make my way across town to the Murphys' little bungalow. Even knowing that Dodie and Frank are beyond gardening can't keep me from believing that they will appreciate the gift, which the nurseryman promised would live for years in its earthenware tub with just a little pruning, a touch of fertilizer. I imagine it homesteaded on the patio, just off the porch outside the kitchen door so Dodie can see it blooming when she sits at the table with Frank.

I'm taking Austin with me when I deliver the housewarming present. Another of my tests, Zoey would probably say, and she'd be halfway right. I can't put into words the panicky swell of distrust which rose in my chest when, coming down from the foothills in the twilight, Austin asked me if I would live with him. Out of nowhere, with no warning, in the middle of a conversation about a pro bono lawsuit he'd filed on behalf of Yolo County migrant workers, for crying out loud, when I'd described to him the single-room hovel that Jorge shared with his father and aunt and uncle.

"It's dark ages," I said, "Jorge sleeps on a pallet on the floor, which means he has to wake up at four when Julian and Lilia and Antonio get up to go to the fields. He's only *six*, Austin."

"Come live with me," Austin said, just like that.

I couldn't answer him. I could only stare out the window at the silhouettes of the oak trees, whose dark outlines against the sunset glow looked like Sierran profiles, as if we were heading into the mountains again instead of returning to the valley. He was serious, though he didn't ask again, and when he flipped Bob Marley into the tape player, I understood the subject was closed for the time being.

Why my reservations about living with this man, this man I know I love beyond measure? I can't blame Henry Talmouth, though I'd like to because he surely deserves blame for something, but I can't say that I ever expected or *wanted* my life joined with Henry Talmouth's in that particular, fixed way. So fear born of disappointment is out. I can't trace it to my upbringing, the total devotion I had for Daddy, unless I use a Freudian lens; besides, Austin is everything—more even—that I would ever hope for in a man, so an Oedipal reading is out. I can't honestly assign responsibility to the marriages I have scrutinized, as clients and as couples, through years and years of field studies. It must be inside me, I think, an anxious congenital dread I can't summon up clearly enough to label.

I want Austin to meet Dodie and Frank because I want him to

understand where it should end up, this grand romantic passion. I want him to appreciate the way Frank's hands find their unconscious way to Dodie's shoulders, how Dodie's voice automatically changes pitch when she drawls out the single syllable of Frank's name. But what I tell Austin on Saturday morning when I pick him up in front of the Leland House is that I want him to carry the heavy pot around the Murphys' bungalow for me.

He leans across the seat to kiss me.

"Of course I will," he says, "I'll be your bracero for the day."

"Two-handed, finally," I say, noticing his right hand is untaped.

He holds his hand to me, palm open.

"All healed—with a scar to remember you by."

"Me? I didn't break the darn glass!"

"Of course you didn't break it . . . you made it all better," he says, brushing the back of his hand against my cheek, extending his fingers across my lips so I can kiss them.

Dodie reaches her hands up to Austin's face as soon as Frank swings open the door. She kisses him, and then me, and Austin shakes hands with Frank.

Austin takes Frank out to the car. Dodie is in the kitchen, filling glasses with iced tea. I watch from the front room window as Austin lifts the pot from the Volvo and sets it down on the sidewalk for Frank to admire. He straddles the pot, hefts it to his chest, and follows Frank around the side of the house to the patio. Dodie is beside me.

"He seems a fine young man, Dolores," she says, motherly, willing to be inquisitive.

"He is, Dodie. He is fine," I reassure her. Hearing the men climbing the stairs to the porch, I take her hand. "Come see what we brought. A little bit of the old days to remember."

In the kitchen, Dodie claps her hands at the sight of the rose. She calls out to Frank to cut her a bloom, right then, for the bud vase she pulls from the china closet in the front room. Frank and

Austin sit down at the kitchen table with us, where we drink iced tea and listen to Dodie's recountings of anecdotes from my childhood. There's the Easter bureau, I tell Austin when we are standing at the door, saying our good-byes. As we walk out to the car, Dodie laughs, a tinkling chime, at something Frank has said.

"You found them the right house," Austin tells me at the curb on Tryon Street. "You found *me* the right house, for that matter. And you could—"

I can hear the question he leaves unsaid: since I love the Leland House, since I love him, isn't moving in the natural choice, won't I think about it?

"She loved the rose," I sidestep his intimations. "And you should have seen the flats of delphinium at Makado's—they'd be perfect off the patio—"

"Too hot yet," he interrupts me with a gruffness I don't recognize. "You need to wait for a real fall before you put in delphiniums."

For the first time in the months we have known each other, something close to anger colors our exchange. But he caps it quickly, with a terse reminder that he's doing dinner for us tonight. I have hurt him with my intentional obfuscation, which he must interpret as misplaced frivolity when it's actually a nervous suspicion of my good luck, the constitutional inheritance from the tragic paradox of entering the world motherless but alive.

Living with Austin is the only thought in my mind as I unlock the apartment door and untwine Milton from my ankles. Absentmindedly I open a can of cat food and rinse Milton's dish and sit down to watch him eat, the tidy smacking sounds he makes the only sensory detail of which I am conscious.

When a person seems to have found the consummation of every romantic expectation and desire, why does caution rear its ugly head? Why can't the person let go and believe in the extension of happiness, the endurance of joy, the perseverance of attachment? Why can't the person, damn it all, have faith in what is happening to her? What makes me so apprehensive about Austin's invitation to live with him, to be his love?

Zoey called me an incurable cynic yesterday, after I had showed a house to a couple whose divorce I predicted. I begged her to wager—my bet was under ten months—but she was too straitlaced to answer me.

"They don't even *listen* to each other, Zoe. He was talking complete bullshit about the turnaround in interest rates and she kept saying, 'But, Ken, where will my fax go?' Their communication is zero, zilch, nada!"

Zoey was unimpressed by my odds making. Worse than that, I think she was disgusted.

"You are," she said primly, whistling through her nose, "an incurable cynic, Dolores."

So I sit in the kitchen of my deliberately unsuitable apartment, Milton wheezing in my lap, and ask myself, is this true? Does cynicism like mine cause people to balk at seizing their own rapture?

I feel as if I need to make a leap of faith, as if I must discard the remnants of exaggerated disappointments garnered over most of a middle-aged lifetime—my father's unexpected death, my early literary withering, my dead-end affair with Henry Talmouth—to step across a chasm of hesitation and enter a terrain as much like make-believe as any I could intentionally design. I want to do it, I can do it, I tell myself, until Milton's lashing tail advises me that I am squeezing him too hard, that I've convinced, if not myself, at least the aging tabby cat in my lap of my sincerity.

In the late afternoon, when I trail the scent of charcoal around the side walk of the Leland House to the patio, I hope that Austin will leave the conversation easy.

"Blackberries," I say to him when his kiss brushes my cheek and I hold the baskets of dark purple fruit up for his inspection.

He takes one between his fingers, studies it, and pops it into his mouth.

"Very nice. With the trout or after?"

He's going out of his way to be accommodating.

"When do *you* want them?" I ask. "You can eat them all now if you'd like—"

"After," he says, turning to fiddle with the grill on the barbecue.

The abrupt transition from feigned graciousness to stony silence tells me I will lose no matter what card I play. If we're going to have this conversation, we may as well have it now, I tell myself. I take the berries into the kitchen, gently roll them into a colander, and let cold water cascade across them. I breathe deeply, turn off the water, and set the berries to drain on the counter.

Austin has left the grill. He squats by the curbing of the slate patio, turning the earth in the flower bed with a hand shovel. It has an unlikely red plastic handle. A slow dawning recognition tells me it's my shovel, the one Austin used for hammering the nails into the plywood sheathing on the front door the day I met him, the same shovel I used to plant Trevor Tuskes's anemones. He stabs the earth and turns it, stabs and turns, with a quick insistent rhythm that delivers to me a subtext I am deciphering even as I sit down on the cool slate beside him and stop his hand when the shovel is buried deep into the loam.

"Don't let's do this," I say. "We can figure this out, don't you think?"

Though he is furious with me, he stands and pulls me to my feet and seats me at the table under the wisteria, whose purple flowers September has turned to heavy seed pods, their blade-shaped bodies wrapped in felt coats. Austin is quickly in and out of the kitchen, bringing to the table a bottle of Chianti, which he uncorks and pours into the gray wine goblets, a full glass for each of us.

"So, Dolores, let's do figure this out. A guy loves you, you say you love him, but it turns you inside out that he wants to live in the same house with you. Is this unreasonable, that I'm perturbed?"

I sip my wine.

"It's not unreasonable that you're perturbed. But if you could try, just listen for a minute, to my perspective, then I wouldn't seem unreasonable, either."

"I'm not Henry Talmouth."

"This isn't about Henry Talmouth, Austin."

"It's got to be about someone."

"It *is* about someone. It's about me. Not some dark figure lurking in my past from whom I've yet to recover. It's about *me*, Austin."

He's trying, I know he is.

"I'm listening," he says, rubbing the tip of his finger around his glass.

The wisteria leaves above our heads rustle. Blocks away, a siren rises and fades. Two dogs bark out a dialogue and quiet.

"It's like this." I shift the wine bottle and lean forward, cradling my arms. "I have this built-in sensor, like a happiness barometer? And when it rises, at the same time that I'm thinking to myself, gee, what a lucky girl I am, something else kicks in and starts warning me watch out, don't get your hopes up. Especially when things seem too good to be true. Whatever it is, it's like a voice scolding me not to count my chickens . . . I believe in you, Austin. I do."

"Your chickens are hatched. They're sitting right here. I don't see—"

"Do you remember I told you about Dr. Chalmers? About those darn dashed hopes? The literary wonder who never was? I've never believed, never let myself believe, in anything that strongly until you . . . I want to let it go, this illogical stuff, but I keep thinking some kind of karma is at work and that if I'm too happy it will disappear, that I'll be—"

Austin leaves his chair and comes to kneel beside me, his arms around my waist, his head against my breast.

"I'm not going to dash your hopes. You *are* a literary wonder, as far as I can see. And, Dolores, I don't truck with karma."

I don't want to truck with karma, either.

I tilt Austin's face to mine, my hands clasping his cheeks.

"Don't you think it's tempting fate? To take something perfect and want to improve on it?"

"It's not perfect until you live here with me. And fate is what you make of life. Somebody else doesn't decide it for you."

"Do you worry that it, what we have, will change?" I ask him, leaning my forehead against his.

"It will only get better . . . people who love one another aren't supposed to live across town from each other and eat breakfast in separate kitchens. . . . I want to wake up with you and cook with you and dance with you and plant trees with you and watch them grow tall as we grow bent and crooked. I want you with me, Dolores."

I watch Austin's dark eyes, the slight upward lift of his eyebrows, his clear forehead, where some day, years and years away, the expression of quizzical concern which he now wears will leave permanent traces of the worry of this moment and of all those to follow, of joy and despair and triumph and misfortune. I know that I want to be with him as each of these moments unfolds, that I want them to be my joys and despairs and triumphs and misfortunes, too, and my wanting this grows stronger than my fear that some giant celestial hand might sweep it all away in one stroke.

"Okay," I tell him. "Okay."

He lays his head in my lap, and I smooth his hair, resting my hand on the nape of his neck so that my fingertips feel his pulse and measure the heartbeats of the man I love.

When you've resolved an immense decision, when the deciding part is behind you and what remains is living with the consequences of your decision, you stop straining forward into the future, into whatever is out there that you can't see, and instead you focus on the present moment, on the feel of the pleasure—or the pain—of the seconds and the minutes in which you are alive. This is what happens to Austin and me on the evening of our engagement. It is as if we are weaving a tapestry that, in better times or in worse, will tie us and all the patterns of our lives together in a meaning larger than ourselves.

We make our evening meal in a comfortable silence as the sun sets against the windows of the Leland House. Inside, I slice the tomatoes that Trevor Tuskes had left for us against the front door and tear lettuce; outside, Austin grills the butterflied trout. When I've set the table and tossed the salad and settled into the seat at what has become my place at the table, he pulls two charred tinfoil-wrapped packages from the grayed charcoal. I raise my eyebrows when he sets them on the platter next to the trout.

"Potatoes. Camping style. None better." He waves the barbecue fork at me. "We need to get up to the mountains before the rain starts. To do some real camping. You game?"

"I'm game." I smile at him, and serve him salad when he deftly hatches a neat cross on my potato.

Have I got a camera, Austin asks me as I hand him my plate and watch him strip the tiny bones from the trout. We could drive up through Yosemite and hike and see the colors turning on the pass. Would I like that? he wants to know.

I would, so we plan the coming weekend and eat a slow dinner. It is nearly ten when we have eaten the last blackberry and gathered up the dishes and carried them into the kitchen. I am rinsing the purple stain from the blackberry bowl when Austin reaches both arms around my waist and hugs me. I lean against him, against his strength and his certainty and the safe boundaries of his arms, and he whispers to me.

"One last dessert," he says.

"I can't eat another—"

"Not food. Wait here. Eyes shut."

I shut my eyes and feel him slip away. I smell the faint perfume of the roses vased on the windowsill. I feel the touch of autumn in the breeze that floats through the kitchen window, just the slightest hint of changing seasons in the edge of coolness. I hear the brushing of the potato vines against the screen. My hands trace the rim of the sink and of the wooden kitchen counter framing it.

"Okay, turn and open," Austin says.

He has bought delphiniums, in blue and white and lavender,

two whole flats of them, their delicate clusters of buds like spires on stalks of fanned leaves.

"Maybe they'll go in now," he says, coming around the table to drape his arm across my shoulders. "Between the two of us gardeners, we ought to be able to make them grow, don't you think?"

"Even if we couldn't, even if we were living in a tent on a forsaken desert, I would choose this," I tell him.

"I know you would," Austin says, circling me with his arms. "I know you would."

The Leland House is my home now, I think, studying the ceiling after Austin has fallen asleep beside me, his arm a sheltering weight across my stomach. I think I've known it as my home in some inarticulate way ever since the flowers tempted me to water them. Austin may not believe in fate or in providence, but what else could have brought us here to these walls, to this bed, to each other.

It's enough that you are here, I tell myself. No point in questioning why or how you arrived. Take this gift you have been given and love the man.

As if to reinforce the commandment I've given myself, a brutal wind shakes the house, one of those wicked gusts the change in seasons produces that belie the Indian summer, the balm of October. The curtain snaps against the bedside table and something clatters to the floor. I listen to Austin's breathing, but it stays even, regular.

I ease from under Austin's arm and, like a blind man searching for a tossed penny, sweep my hands across the floor. I pick up the fallen wood-framed photograph and step next to the window so I can study it in the rays from the street lamp.

It is the original of Austin's backpacking photograph, the one downstairs on the bookshelves, the one he had enlarged because he says it reminds him of his father. The glass has cracked. I promise myself I will have it replaced so Austin will never know that it's been broken. A wife already, I am thinking.

Another gust blows against the house. I lay the frame facedown on the bedside table and crawl beneath the covers to snuggle against Austin once more.

His form is warm and solid.

But I am shivering.

CHAPTER TEN

Tell all the truth but tell it slant —

Tell all the Truth but tell it slant—
Success in Circuit lies
Too bright for our infirm Delight
The Truth's superb surprise

As Lightning to the Children eased
With explanation kind
The Truth must dazzle gradually
Or every man be blind—

EMILY DICKINSON 1868

ON MY DESK, I have spread out my camera and four rolls of film.
Next to the Leica, Jason Loman's paper sits on top of my stack of
graded work, the last remaining essay to read from my ten-thirty
section. Once I've finished it, I will load for the drive up Tioga Pass
and call Dolores to remind her to set her clock, no fooling around
this time, so we can make an early start. High clouds have clung
to the Sierras all day; the potential for rain during our weekend
makes planning more complicated than I would like. Sleeping out
seemed like a good idea, but if it's raining in Yosemite Valley, we
might want to skip the sleeping bags and head over to Lee Vining
and a dry hotel room.

I pick up Jason's paper and lean back in my chair, lifting my
feet to the desktop, careful of the Leica. After two weeks of classes,
I'm able to match most of my students' names to their faces, so the
onerous chore of attendance-taking is something I now do quickly,

without relying on the antiquated habit of seating charts or using class time to read the long roster of names. For me, reviewing their first papers has fleshed out their identities, configured their voices and their aptitudes. Elaine Towers, the morose dark-haired woman who sits stony-faced directly in front of the podium, writes with a decisive clarity that some of my colleagues would do well to imitate. Everett Burrise, the lanky guy in sloppy surfer shorts whom I suspected of sleeping through the last twenty minutes of Monday's lecture, not only heard every point that we covered but dared to offer some compelling independent analysis, as well: evidence that he's reading—and thinking—far beyond the minimal requirements of a first-year contracts course. As a reward to myself for my steady progress through the thick sheaf of arguments, I have purposely left Jason's paper until last because he is so engaging, so clever without being off-putting. He demonstrates that he's an ace writer, too, I see as I scan the first page, fast becoming my star student, my Jorge, I think. On the long ride up the pass tomorrow, I will tell Dolores about Jason, and she will tell me about Jorge and the progress she's making with the second-graders' ballads.

The children will rise to expectation, she said to me yesterday, patronizing, when I doubted her use of "The Highwayman" as a model.

"But will they stick with it for seventeen verses?" I questioned her.

"Maybe not seventeen verses, professor. But they can tell stories, yes? The idea is to anticipate success," she harangued in one of her characteristic yet startling philosophical inconsistencies. "You need to change your point of view, buddy. The right to fail has been replaced by the prerogative to excel."

She put her hand to her temple, then pointed at me. "Couldn't resist the opportunity for pomposity."

"Pompous or not, you bring out the best in those kids," I told her. And added, because I couldn't resist and because it's true, "And in me," which earned me a kiss and produced a surge of gratitude that Dolores, mute or pompous, solemn or frivolous, is mine, that her eccentric commentaries will soon become a constant of my daily life.

I reflect on her talent for translating the abstract theoretical complexities of learning theory to the concrete crayon exercises she conducts in the bare-bones classroom at the Hispanic Community Center. It's an ironic gift of her profession, she told me, rather than the legacy of her one-time avocation. She went on to suggest that reading law, like poetry, ought to be a concrete exertion also, an intriguing insight that I am mulling when a quick series of taps rattles the glass of the front door.

"You did say Friday, early evening, didn't you?" says Zoey when I pull open the door and usher her inside.

"I did—I was upstairs, reading arguments. Come in, let me show you around."

"Dolores was right. You've performed a miracle with this house." She steps to the wall and runs her hand across the blue-lined wallpaper. "The paper is perfect—I confess I never shared Dolores's faith the house could be renovated—"

"Dolores told me—you thought she'd have better luck selling a bare lot."

"Seeing this makes me glad I was wrong." Zoey smiles. "That doesn't happen very often—being glad about it. Or being wrong—"

"Take a look at the rest."

Zoey moves to the curved windows that fit the base of the corner cupola and pulls the lace curtains aside.

"Dolores's choice," I say when she remarks on the fabric. "I wanted to keep the house light."

She follows me to the kitchen and stands with her hands on the sink counter, surveying the garden outside.

She turns to me and speaks slowly, as if she's thinking of something else. "I can see why a woman would love what you've done with this house."

"A *woman* did much of it," I say, irritated without knowing why, except that in some odd way at this moment Zoey reminds me of Clair Mariani.

We are trapped in an uneasy silence following my shortness. To break it, I offer Zoey a beer, a glass of wine, an iced coffee.

"I did want to see the house, Austin. But I came to see you, really. As Dolores's closest friend, her family representative, you could say."

I choose wine and pour two glasses of zinfandel, setting them deliberately on the flat iron mark on the kitchen table.

"Sit down, Zoey," I say. "You're inspecting the suitor? Checking that his intentions are honorable?"

I've embarrassed her.

"Not that. I really want to talk about Dolores . . . to protect her interests?"

"I fully intend to protect her interests. I want her to live here, with me, forever and ever. I don't see what you're—"

"I want her to live here, too. That's just it—I want her to be as happy as she deserves to be. She can be irreverent and crusty and impossible, but in some ways she's childish, Austin. Emotionally, I mean." Zoey twists a thin gold chain at her neck, then pulls at a teardrop earring.

"Do you think I haven't figured her out? That I don't know who she is?"

"I didn't mean to imply that. I just want you to appreciate her. She's special, she's one of a kind . . ."

She stops, averts her eyes, wrings her hands in her lap, and I suddenly understand what she's trying to tell me.

"I'm no Henry Talmouth, Zoey. I'm not built that way."

Zoey sighs and looks up at me. "I'm glad, Austin. For both your sakes, I'm glad. This is a happy time, then." She rises and sets her full glass on the counter by the sink.

The phone rings, relieving us both of having to say more.

"I love the house," she says, stepping to the parlor.

The phone rings a second time.

"Get that—I can find my way out."

The phone rings a third time. I pick it up and cup my hand over the mouthpiece.

"Zoey," I call after her, "I'm not anybody you need to worry about on Dolores's account."

She returns to the kitchen doorway and gestures to the phone.

"I know," she says, backing from the kitchen, her arms raised, flags of capitulation.

"Excuse me, hello, Austin Barclay here," I say into the phone after the front door has clicked shut.

"Austin? Dr. Hindari."

The line seems to have gone dead.

"Dr. Hindari?"

"Austin? Are you there?" The sober cadences of his accented voice rise and fall like tolling bells.

"Yes."

"I have some news regarding the blood tests we redid. Some hard news, I'm afraid."

My first thought is that I must have diabetes, the disease that killed my maternal grandmother. Or that I must have picked up hepatitis from the reckless decision I made to drink creek water when I hiked into Shotgun Lake in early summer, my first week out from New York. Such a snowpack, I had rationalized, that it wouldn't kill me to—

"—rerunning the tests because we thought there'd been a lab error, but we've eliminated that possibility now. You're testing positive for HIV, Austin."

If a person is really blessed, really lucky in life, he never feels the earth fall away beneath his feet as if the planet is trying to hurl him off into space, to shrug him into some black hole whose existence he never truly believes until he finds himself hurtling through it, the breath being vacuumed from his lungs. If a person is really blessed, he never feels himself sinking into a black ocean so deep the memory of sunlight is erased by its own absence, his lungs filling with the dark water that makes the prospect of breathing as faint a possibility as the sun's rays through the ebony depths, their frail, watery tendrils like the tail of some underwater meteor whose proof of existence is simultaneously the assurance of its extinction.

If a person is really blessed, he never feels the lightning strike that lays him out, a cool corpse.

Dr. Hindari's voice is mesmerizing. Astonishing, he's saying, given the absence of high-risk behaviors in my profile . . . could I determine where or when the virus was acquired? Whether I hear him or not doesn't matter because the litany is ritual: a singsong requiem of AZT successes, heterosexual support groups, cautionary procedures, notification of sexual partners. When he reaches the summation, when he's offered me the requisite words of comfort and advice, when I've rested the phone in its place and my hands are hanging limp at my sides, I can only think of escaping, of running from what I carry inside me.

And of what I may have given to Dolores.

I pick up the phone once again, the instrument of death, and dial Dolores's apartment. The staccato ring repeats like gunshots. I don't know what I will say, how I *can* say what I must. Dolores's taped voice saves me.

"Dolores Meredith. Leave your name and number, and I'll return the call when I get in."

My words are dull, the speech of a paralytic.

"This is Austin . . . Something unavoidable . . . inescapable . . . has come up. I need to leave for the weekend . . . I'll be in touch."

The pile of gear next to the front door finds its way into the Jeep, the lights in the Leland House are extinguished, the front door locked, the key replaced under the loose brick in the border of the oval beds. Some stranger to myself oversees this departure, the forced exodus of a man from his soul, the abdication of all that supplies motive and meaning to my life.

The stranger propels me down Highway 99. On the outskirts of Stockton, I am returned to myself by the flashing red lights of a black and white, which parallels the Jeep like a shadow. When I register its presence, I realize that I don't know how long it's been mated to the Jeep on the dark southbound highway. The speedometer reads eighty-five. I slow to sixty, then shift down and pull onto the gravel shoulder. Oleanders brush the passenger side door. Poisonous, I tell myself in a moment of misplaced clarity that illuminates madness. Don't want to eat the leaves.

The patrolman's voice bellows from a bullhorn behind the Jeep.

"Get out of the car—slowly—hands against the hood. Both hands."

It's easy to follow these commands, to do what I'm told without question. The patrolman approaches, the glare of his high beams creating a giant moving shade of a man who darkens my face before he reaches my side.

"I'm going to pat you down, fella," he says, and I feel his hands run down my arms, my legs. "Then you're going to explain why you've been doing eighty for the last five miles. I've been lit up behind you for four of them."

He steps in close, inhales, and tells me I can put my arms down and show him a license.

I find my wallet, the Jeep's registration. He writes out a ticket as he conducts a cursory sobriety test, hand to nose, ten steps heel-to-toe.

"Just a speed demon by nature, huh?" he says, handing me the ticket.

He leaves me with an admonition about speed limits and penalties and is walking back to his cruiser when I break down, my head hanging, my hands clutching at my shoulders, great wretched sobs wracking me bent.

The scatter of gravel against a wheel rim tells me he's returned.

"It's a speeding ticket, for Christ's sake," he says, taking my shoulder. "Get a hold of yourself, big guy. It's starting to rain anyway."

He opens the Jeep's door and pushes me into the seat, capping my head with his hand in the peculiar protective gesture of arresting officers.

"Go home, friend," he says through the window, leaning close to my face. "I don't know what your troubles are, but this is not a night for you to be out."

It is raining full force when I pull off the road at Tuolumne Meadows and shut off the Jeep's lights. The raindrops drum against the roof and the windshield, curtaining what lies outside. I could find a cabin at Mather, where the ranger at the gate said cancellations have left vacancies. I could drive out of the park and find a hotel. I could go home.

I make none of these paltry choices because they don't in the end change anything, the outcome of what having this disease is sure to mean. Instead, I sit in the Jeep, my head leaning against the cold windowpane, and run through my mind a thousand what if's, a thousand more why me's. By morning, when the rain has let up and a shroud of fog blankets the meadows, I have calculated that I had to have acquired the virus from Julie Tyndel, Clair Mariani's final, failed gift, during the long snowed-in weekend we had spent together nearly sixteen months ago, when she told me it was all right, she was on the pill, when all we had in common for two days was sex because she wouldn't put on snowshoes. How many exposures does it take for a man, I wonder, how many half-rate couplings cost me what I've lost, what I've yet to lose. I believe that she didn't know, and when I recall up her haggard face the night of my farewell dinner in New York, I realize that she may not know now, that it's up to me to tell her.

And to tell Dolores.

Who may be infected.

Who may not be infected.

Whose heart I am going to break one way or another.

The Jeep's engine turns over, and I double back and take the turnoff to the May Lake trailhead in second gear, the wisps of rising fog disguising what should be familiar terrain. I park—the sole car in the narrow lot—and strap my down bag onto the new backpack, stuffing the loose pieces of my futile packing into its pockets. Last night in Woodland seems an eternity away from these clammy dawn hours under the dripping trees; the mind which composed the scrupulously categorized list and checked the items laid out on the oak table of the Leland House kitchen in preparation of this trip is a foreigner to the mind inside my head. All it wants—this tightened mass of muscle—is to split its seams, to explode, to run, to climb and never stop.

Climb is what I do. I heft the pack onto my shoulders and set out for the lake. I can head up the trail beyond the inlet and reach the high camp at Glen Aulin from there. This time of year, this high up, I won't find anyone else on the trail. For five hours I walk, a hard pace. Despite the cool air and the heavy low clouds blocking the sun, sweat has soaked through my flannel shirt and sweatshirt and the lined parka I've layered on. As long as my feet move, one after the other, I can stop the drumbeats in my brain. Tell her, lose her, lose her, tell her, my pulse harps if I slow my strides.

Exhaustion thwarts me before I reach the Glen Aulin camp. Thunder cracks the sky above my head, above the Silver Firs and Mountain Pines that umbrella the trail. I sink to my knees and lean against the pack, too weary to slide the straps off my burning shoulders. A sheet of cold rain slaps against my face. Every muscle aches. This is better, I think, than the wasp buzz of thoughts that drove me up the mountain. Ice silences feeling better than fire, numbness better than fever. I am pinned to the earth by the weight of the pack. How long I sit, splayed against the granite outcropping, I can't know, except that the light lowers against the west and leaves the outlines of rock and tree circling me like the walls of an ancient fortress. When I'm soaked through, the voice of reason nudges me up and back against the trunk of a Mountain Hemlock, the drooping sprays of its branches a natural tent. I shake out my rain gear and bag, draping a plastic tarp over my head when I twist out of the soaked clothes and squeeze myself into the zippered down. I sit against the trunk of the tree, enveloped in the plastic, and listen to the moaning wind playing the high branches.

The storm has passed by morning. With my eyes shut and my head tilted against the hemlock's base so that my matted hair catches in its rough bark, I know what I have to do. I have to walk down this trail, drive back up the highway to Woodland, and take Dolores in to Dr. Hindari's clinic for testing. I will face what follows—whatever it is—but I will face it head-on. I will not run anymore. I open my eyes and follow the leafy branches of the tree up the trunk, up to the vanishing point where the narrow tip touches the ceiling of the backwashed sky. A place inside me, deep within a nucleus that is not glacial yet, remembers my father teaching me about these hardy, faithful conifers, their stoic patience through the Sierran snows, when even the saplings, after a six-month burial in snow and ice, emerge from entombment unscathed, their leafy foliage defiant ornaments of spring.

I *will* face it head-on. I know what I have to do.

The treacherous downhill footing makes the homeward trail slow, my footholds cautious on the litter of rock, some of which is gullied by last night's thunderstorm. It is Sunday midafternoon by the time I reach the Jeep, and I feel the chill in my bones from the severe night, the clammy shirt on my back. The grumbling in my stomach reminds me I've not eaten since Friday evening. Some intellectual physiology my mind understands but the cells of my body are so far ignorant of tells me I need to warm up, to eat well, to rest.

I put the heater on high and drive to Curry Village, where the cafeteria is open and warm. I load a tray with hot food: mashed potatoes, fried chicken, green beans, white bread and butter, whole milk.

"Hiked up an appetite?" says the gray-haired checker, running my total.

I nod and hand her a bill.

"Wish I could eat like that. Got to watch my cholesterol, these days. Creeps up on you . . . those triglycerides . . . ," she continues to herself, handing me my change.

I don't know whether to laugh or to cry at the black humor symbolized by my laden platter of institutional food. I can't bring myself to tell her I don't foresee heart disease in my medical prognosis.

The duty of eating recalls to me other duties, and a checklist grows in my conscience. I must call Dolores and Julie Tyndel and Dr. Hindari.

Dolores first.

I'm going to need to be the calm one, I tell myself as I drive up the Central Valley to Woodland, because I've had forty-eight hours to live with my toxic knowledge. Which means, after I've showered, twice listened to the phone tapes of the increasingly angry messages Dolores left throughout the weekend, and stared at my desk for an hour, that it isn't fair to call her at next to midnight on a Sunday evening. My news wants publication in the full light of day, not the dead of night.

In the morning, shaving, I study myself in the mirror: the cast of my eyes, the color of my skin. You can't tell by looking, I think, and recognize that it might take years before the onset of disease touches the essential texture of my working life. When I push my razor onto the second shelf of the medicine cabinet against a half-empty, shrink-wrapped box of condoms, I can hear Dolores preaching to me, a pretend old-lady diction from my unmade bed, "I ain't Aunt Emmabelle yet." I say a prayer of thanks that we have never, not once, failed at using what we believed with grown-up certitude to be protection against conception. It may in the end, if Dolores is luckier than I, be a defense against death. There's some comfort in this, and the comfort sturdies me when I sit down at my desk, apologize mentally to Jason Loman—one guilt I don't deserve—for his ungraded essay, and dial Dolores's number.

The machine answers.

I hang up.

I dial again.

The machine answers.

This time, I leave a message: "Dolores, it's Austin. I need to see you . . . a serious reason. I'll try you again from school. If I don't reach you, I'll be back in Woodland at one and come by the office."

It's harder and harder to put this off, but a half-day longer means a half-day reprieve from renunciation of hope for a life with the woman I have grown to cherish above all else, a woman who will have every right in the world to turn tail and run from the messenger who bears the message in his blood.

My watch reads 7:45, which makes it late morning in New York. I open my address book and find the number of Bookman's, the law firm for whom Julie Tyndel was working when I left New York.

After a crisp voice barks out "Bookman's Law," I offer my name and my position before asking to speak with Julie.

"Ms. Tyndel has taken a medical leave." The voice softens. "She can be reached at her apartment, I believe."

I feel as if I am digging at bedrock, but I find Julie's home number and dial.

"Hello?" It's a female voice, older, midwestern, not Julie's.

"I'm an acquaintance—a friend—of Julie's. Austin Barclay. I wanted to speak with her—"

The sharp voice clips mine. "We took Julie to the hospital yesterday. This is her mother speaking. What do you want?"

"Is it possible to speak with her? Do you know how long she'll be in?"

"Not possible. And I don't know." A muffling slurs the connection; the voice returns. "Didn't you know she has pneumonia?"

The phone slams down then, as though Julie's mother has expended her store of forced niceties.

I know what I need to know.

One call down.

CHAPTER ELEVEN

After great pain, a formal feeling comes ——

♪♫

After great pain, a formal feeling comes—
The Nerves sit ceremonious, like Tombs—
The stiff Heart questions was it He, that bore,
And Yesterday, or Centuries before?

The Feet, mechanical, go round—
Of Ground, or Air, or Ought—
A Wooden way
Regardless grown,
A Quartz contentment, like a stone—

This is the Hour of Lead—
Remembered, if outlived,
As Freezing persons, recollect the Snow—
First—Chill—then Stupor—then the letting go—

EMILY DICKINSON 1862

HE MAKES ME feel the way Henry did.

Only one hundred times worse.

One thousand times more furious. Because it matters now. And because I never expected this from Austin: the casual brush-off, the irresponsibility, the ex post facto explanation indefinitely postponed. "See you at one," he leaves on my machine when I am enmeshed in a morning meeting with Arinda Mesa and the Volunteer Steering Committee, then sails blithely off to his lecture as if I haven't been out of my mind for two days.

"I hope it's nothing I said," Zoey murmurs to me after I storm into the office late this morning, railing against the infidelity of men.

She stops me in my tracks.

"What do you mean?"

Zoey can't dissemble, not to save her soul. She blushes from the neck of her white blouse up to the crown of her forehead, a confessional rash that sinks my heart as it rises across her face.

"Zoey, what have you done?" I lean over her desk.

Zoey covers her face with her hands.

"Zoey?"

"I'm going to tell you," she says, uncovering her face. "It's not awful the way you're thinking."

"Tell me now." I sit down across the desk from Zoey like a disgruntled client.

"I went to look at the house Friday night. You remember? And I said a few things that may have . . . may have . . ."

"Zoey."

"Made him angry. A little." She pulls at her earring.

"What!"

"I told him you were special, that he ought to appreciate you . . . I was there as your best friend, Dolores."

"Oh my God." I push myself away from the desk, a movement so sudden that Zoey starts. "Zoey, I'm all grown up. I can do this by myself. You don't need to run interference for—"

"It wasn't interference. All I said was that I cared about you and that I expected him to. That's all."

"Oh my God." I stand up from the desk and reach over to the ficus tree, pulling polished dark leaves off one by one, strewing them over my feet and the floor. "He probably thought I'd hired you . . . as an insurance salesman . . . oh my God."

You like to think you really know someone at some fixed point in time, after so many months, so many weekends, so many nights. When the cut of his chin and the laugh wrinkles at his eyes have grown as familiar to you as your own image in the mirror, you like to think that by knowing the person you can shield yourself from nasty surprises: a man who cheats on his income tax, a disconsolate drinker, a secret slob who leaves the toilet seat up and his beard in your razor. I wanted to trust I knew everything about Austin, every possible reaction he might have to particular people, precise ideas. I guess I was working so hard at subduing my reservations that I had forgotten he might have some of his own, might not appreciate a visit from a well-meaning but intrusive screening committee.

But he shouldn't have left me in the lurch. No matter what. And how could anything Zoey have said or done change who I am, who he is, and what we've pledged?

I tell Zoey she's going to have to handle the drive-bys with the clients who are coming in at eleven-thirty, and I toss a bundle of listings on her desk.

"Where are you going?"

"I'm going to Davis, to talk to Austin. To figure this out."

"Dolores, I apologize. I didn't—"

"It's all right, Zoe." I pat her arm. "I'm not upset with *you.*"

The Volvo rattles down the freeway to Davis. I plan to find King Hall, Austin's office, his classroom if necessary, and tell him what I think: that standing me up for a good reason is one thing, but leaving me on ice for three days is too reminiscent of Henry Talmouth for me ever to handle with good grace.

The lot closest to the law school is crowded with students vying for parking spaces and more students attempting to exit. A grim dark-haired woman walks by the Volvo and points to her car, a little Honda. Take the space, her hands are telling me, so I wait for her to back out, then roll the Volvo into her slot. The lot resounds with gunning engines, slamming doors. As I'm turning from the Volvo to make my way between the chain of outgoing cars to the curb, four alleys away a dark head catches my eye. It's Austin, slipping behind the wheel of his Jeep. I wave to him, call out his name, but his window blocks my summons and he doesn't see me.

By the time I'm in the Volvo and awaiting my turn at the stop sign on Arboretum, he is gone.

Gone home. Just like he said. To swing by the office at one.

I pull up to the Leland House; there's no sign of the Jeep. On the lustrous oak floor beyond the leaded glass lie Austin's gutted backpack, a half-rolled sleeping bag, a black camera satchel. The front door is unlocked, but I sit on the bottom porch step anyway, the better to play lookout. The oval beds at my feet need tending, the layered leaf-fall from the neighborhood trees sodden with the weekend's rain. Leave them long enough and the leaves will mulch themselves into a fertile carpet, germinating the invisible seed pods sunken below the soil without any forecasting from nervous gardeners. I realize, with the curious detachment that intervenes in the midst of ultimate distraction, that we haven't settled what winter bulbs we are going to put down once we rake: Austin lobbying for a mix of yellow crocus, white snowdrops, blue hyacinths; my own preference a mass of hyacinths alone.

He sees me when he pulls up behind my car. He sits, his head leaning against the wheel, as if he's dreading the recrimination he knows is coming, as if he doesn't deserve it. Then, slow motion, he's opening the door and pushing through the gate, walking up the bricks, standing in front of me.

What I notice when he crosses the bricked pathway without a greeting, what chills me to the bone with premonition when he raises his eyes to me, is that the boyishness is dissipated. The mouth which opens as if to speak is not the one that sang with Bruce Springsteen when Austin held me in his arms and danced me across the unfinished wood floors of the Leland House. The person in front of me is not the Austin who laid me down against a pallet upstairs and remade my life by loving me. The leaden man loosening his tie and sitting down next to me without touching is an interloper, a trespasser.

"Were you really so far off the beaten track you couldn't reach me?" I say after he has flayed the head of a spent zinnia, spraying the spear-shaped seeds across his knees, which he brushes clean, carefully, before cupping his hands on his knees.

"Can't you even say you're sorry? Do you know how crummy it feels to sit waiting for the phone to ring when you don't know if you've been stood up or shut down or what in hell is going on?"

The strong hands tighten, white knuckling.

"God damn you, Austin, I don't deserve this." I stand up, three days added to seven years' worth of woman scorned, and stamp my foot on the wooden step.

"Talk to me! You've made a stalker out of me, for Christ's sake. The least you could do is talk to me!"

As if some fairy godmother has waved a wand and restored order to our besieged kingdom, the stranger becomes my Austin, his face breaking in sorrow, his arms taking me to his chest, his voice sobbing into my hair.

"I'm so sorry, I'm so sorry, I'm so sorry," he is saying, over and over and over again until I stop him with my palm against his lips.

"It's okay . . . we'll have another weekend. What happened? Tell me what happened. It'll be okay. We'll make it okay." In non-sensical patter—the gibbered solace of a good witch—I soothe him, brushing his too-long hair with my hand, wiping the tears streaming down his cheeks.

"Dolores," he says, trapping my hands against his chest. "I love you more than all the world . . . remember that I love you more than all the world. Whatever becomes of us, I will love you."

In this moment when I am frighted to my bones my stilled blood conjures up a malign mandala of omens: Austin's wry comment, months ago, between sets at Zeke's Dance Palace, about being drawn west, drawn home; his bloody hand, the practice death; the cracked glass on the bedside photograph.

"I've tested positive for HIV, Dolores."

The fairy godmother flees. The good witch melts.

No breath, no oxygen, no pulse.

"We need to see if I've given it to you."

I am semiconscious of Austin's hand on my wrist guiding me

through the front door, seating me at the oak table, where a full glass of red wine sits centered on the flat iron burn. I am vaguely aware of his conversation on the telephone, the familiar rise and fall of his voice. He could be talking to a colleague or a repairman; the topic could be California tort law or the erratic plumbing patterns upstairs. This time, that place, and thank you, sir.

But he isn't.

He's arranging our fate—my fate—with Dr. Hindari.

My eyes fall to the polished oak floor beneath my feet where, weeks ago, with my bare hands and a dish towel, I scrubbed away the poisoned blood of the lover with whom I've traded one hundred tender intimacies, none made as appalling to me now as his blood puddling, wiped away by these trembling hands.

Hands that I am always bruising or scraping or cutting.

Hands that even now, as they quiver in my lap, are scabbed on two knuckles.

There was so much blood that the bucket I filled with rinse water turned burgundy. And I—I dipped and wrung and swabbed with my bare hands until the golden oak shone because I'd heard that if blood is allowed to soak into wood it never washes free. That's why it's so hard to sell a murder scene, a broker at Parker told me my first year, hoping to joke his way into my bed. Clients claim they can see the blood patterns. And then they want to talk about the crime. And then they want a discount for bad vibrations.

I can't see the blood anymore, but I can see my fingers erasing the trail of ruby drops, every one, all the way from the front door to the sink, where I held Austin's hand and his blood wouldn't stop and he bled against my opened palms, my bare hands—

"We need to go, Dolores," Austin whispers, kneeling beside me.

I stand up. He reaches for my elbow.

"Please!" Reflex whips my arms around my shoulders. Instinct lashes a single word: "Don't."

"Dolores?"

"All that blood . . . all your blood . . . it covered my hands . . . my hands were wet with it . . . with your blood . . ."

I might have slapped him, a surprise backhand hard against his blanched face, a response so unlike the Dolores he thinks he loves that it would redefine me as irreversibly as he has done himself. Or my open palm might mark his face—a red stigmata, a blunt birth-mark—all gone by tomorrow. But my words—I would take them back if my body would let me, I would swallow them whole—they have committed a cruelty my hands never could.

I lift the glass from its station on the charred scar and pour it down the sink. Its twin sits on the counter, and I pour it down, too, rinsing the sink well with cold water, a cheap disguise of the fact that I can't leave this house before scrubbing my hands. I tuck the glasses into the dishwasher and look up to see Austin watching, his eyes swelling with tears.

We climb into the Jeep and ride together—a funeral procession of two inside the gleaming, whirring casket—retracing our route down the freeway.

Austin speaks only once during the merciless pilgrimage. "We used a condom every time," he says, his hands tight around the wheel. "I do know that."

He repeats this soft-spoken mantra to Dr. Hindari, a stern white-suited vampire who dabs at my skin and draws my blood. I watch every step of the cold process without blinking: the needle sinking into my swollen vein, the soundless suction of the collection tube, the rubber digits capping miniature glass cylinders of a darker hue than the wine I washed down the drain of the Leland House. When the pristine sash of a flesh-colored Band-Aid seals my arm and the scratched labels bearing my name certify my transition into novitiate or survivor, Dr. Hindari speaks.

"We'll ask the lab to run these tests as soon as possible." He glances at the heavy gold watch on his wrist. "It's nearly four now . . . we should have the results in twenty-four hours . . . say five tomorrow." He pauses, locks eyes with Austin, then looks at me. "Is there a number I can reach—"

"Mine," Austin and I say together, our matched syllables leaving a single echo in the small lab room.

We both want to claim this sorry proclamation, a sympathetic agreement on terms. I leave the apartment's number with Dr. Hindari, and we make our solemn procession to the Jeep. Once the motor turns and Austin pulls away from the stucco clinic—I am seething with hate for its antiseptic air, its blind-disguised windows—we are relieved of any obligation to etiquette. I reach my hand to the radio dial and turn up the sound. Static crackles; then a saxophone riff bursts from the speakers, filling the car with a darkening elegy.

In tragedy there comes a passover between shock and awareness, a sill over which one steps from grand drama to the bland resumption of the mundane. The mother who has lost her only child to a head-on collision finds herself turning from the uniformed officer in her living room to make a cup of tea. The booted soldier on the smoking death field will think to shoulder his canteen before the backward entrenchment made over the fallen bodies of his comrades. Following official notice of the likelihood that one may have acquired the human immunodeficiency virus, the vital human being will be called to the necessary ceremonies of common life.

"Have you had lunch?" I ask Austin, the first words I've spoken to him since our departure from Woodland.

He shakes his head, no.

"Are you hungry?" I ask.

"How about you?"

"I could eat something . . ." I watch his face. "We . . . should eat, shouldn't we?"

Austin nods. With a stillborn clarity, I read the gratitude in his eyes: for my question, for my use of "we" to describe us, for a wellspring of nobility he relies on me to divine and to draw from. How can he trust in my goodness at this moment when my yellow palms itch against my skirt with the compulsion to be washed? When did I earn this absolute faith of his that yokes me in my seat? Why am I now charged with disproving his belief that I can bear this?

He takes an exit signaled by the ubiquitous Denny's, twenty-four-hour satisfaction guaranteed. Inside, it rushes from him, the novella, no, short story, too short for chapters even. Between the ice water and the menus, between the plastic basket of white rolls and the perky artificial salad—one slivered tomato, one nicked radish allotted each plate—the narrative unfolds: the snowflakes against the window, the pressed-sawdust logs burning cheerily in the miniature woodstove, the up-and-coming Berkeley-degreed lawyer (she didn't think to bring boots!), and the heterosexual comfort of every woman's savior—the villain birth control pill.

When Austin reaches the conclusion and the pseudo-spaghetti is steaming into our faces, I see that our story has a climax yet unwritten. At five tomorrow in my tiny apartment, when Milton's mellow eyes will wink at the trilling telephone, a hand will reach for the receiver and the story will peak. Except that we have leapfrogged the climax and are drafting the denouement, the falling action, as we prod the swollen strings of pasta and avoid looking into each other's eyes. Because something always happens after the final page of the written story, doesn't it? Because the happily-ever-after sentence cannot encompass the ripples, the aftershocks of what took place way, way back, on pages two and seven and thirty-eight, so far back the reader might easily have forgotten.

"I want to be with you when he calls," Austin says as the hissing skirt of the wide-hipped waitress retreats and leaves us an abbreviated moment of privacy.

"You were alone."

"Alone wasn't a good way to hear that kind of news."

"I've had to move the poetry workshop to Tuesdays. The center needs the classroom for new baby checkups."

"You'll have to cancel."

"I will cancel." I tear a packet of NutraSweet into shreds, spilling the white granules onto the tablecloth, marshaling them into a tiny pyramid with my fingers. With a runaway viciousness born of my own panic, I say, "I wouldn't miss it. It'll be the phone call of a lifetime."

Austin covers his face with his hands. At the inside base of his thumb, I can see the tip of his scar, a fresh purple wheal. I wrapped that hand with mine, bravely, foolishly staunching its blood flow in the sunlit kitchen of the Leland House. As much an act of love as any that we have made, its remembrance cuts me to the bone with horror. Something deep inside me, something more kind and more selfless than the cauterized nerves on which I am running, tells me I should reach my hand out and stroke his cheek with my curled fingers. Except that, weighted as it is with fright, I can't will my arm to lift.

"Everything all right here, hon? More coffee?" The blowzy waitress returns. "You want to try the devil's food for dessert?"

Austin rises and bolts from the booth, disappearing around the lobby corner.

"He feeling all right, hon? Everything all right here?"

I stuff money into her hand and stand, disengaging myself from the vinyl seat, edging around the uniformed bosom.

I look into the painted face and grimace. I lie.

"He'll be all right."

Austin's eyes are shut as I drive the Jeep into Woodland, parking it behind the house, in front of the little shed that he has made his wood shop. We walk to the curb side by side, our feet rustling the leaves. As I reach for the Volvo's door, he breaks the long silence.

"Come in, Dolores. Please." He manages a crooked smile. "We're the same people we were a week ago . . . please."

I look down at my feet, my dress-to-impress navy heels I put on so long ago—this morning—as a convincing statement to the Volunteer Steering Committee that we should find space to let the poetry workshops continue. Don't mess with me, I was hoping my dark suit said. I mean business.

I raise my eyes to Austin. "I can't."

"Dolores?"

"Austin! Nothing's the same! And I . . . I am so afraid . . ."

I watch his hands. I will them to keep from reaching for me. They hang at his sides.

"Of me . . . Dolores?"

I don't look at Austin's face. I can't look. I might see what I can't bear: the reflection of self-interest, the confirmation of an atavistic egoism, a human self made animal.

And Austin would see—Austin would see that I am less than what he thought, a contraction of disease he doesn't deserve. We're not the same people; we've been changed beyond the scope of calibration. Because when nature or God or fate prescribes for us the cessation of joy, we are forever altered. I have become a woman he has never known: whose every cell cries flee! save yourself! A woman who has been gutted by fear, by these sorrows multiplying, mutating with every word we speak. A black selfishness which won't be stifled turns me away from this man, my lover, who pleads for what I can't give—not now, not today! Even as I turn, I feel an ugliness swelling in my stingy heart, the dark coals of shame . . . what Austin mistook for diamonds.

I shake my head and choke on my sentence. "I need . . . to go home. Please." I slide behind the wheel and close the door, the solid clinch of the hinge like a wrought iron gate swinging safely shut behind me.

"Tomorrow. At four," I tell him, rolling up the window.

That evening I mourn my refusal to comfort or be comforted, when I belatedly remember to feed Milton in my cold apartment, when I crawl beneath the rumpled sheets of my bed without brushing my teeth, when I fall into a fitful sleep so troubled that Milton keens, a solitary drawn-out wail. In the tortured predawn minutes, when the murmur of the leaf-sweeping truck lures Milton from my pillow to the windowsill and I stand under water so hot I can believe it sterilizes my scalding skin, I grovel in my own fear. I study my hands: the fingertips puckered by the beating downpour, the lines on my palms, the clumsy knuckles, the chipped fingernails. Again and again, I witness these awkward hands made talented, merciful tools by a desire that buckled us, breathless, day after day. Over and over I watch myself swabbing the trail of blood that lead me from passion to where I am now, steeped in self-centered agony, shuddering, sinking to the floor of the tub until the water runs cold.

Somehow, I live—such a weighted word!—through Tuesday. I call Zoey and leave the office in her hands. For most of the gray hours that follow, my hands seek consolation against Milton's fur and the vibration of his purr. I am sitting on the couch wrapped in Dodie Murphy's afghan, Milton heavy upon my legs, when Austin knocks at close to four.

"Did you teach today?" I ask him when he finally settles into my abandoned nest on the couch.

"I did." Safe from contagion, immune to the torpor following fright that has claimed his mistress, Milton leaps onto the couch, turns his heavy body twice, and eases onto Austin's lap. "I don't know what else to do. I can't sit . . . I don't want to think. . . . There's something to be said for going through the motions." He strokes Milton, outlining the silky white patch, the warrior's trophy.

"You?" he asks.

"Me? I can't stop thinking. . . . My mind runs in circles . . ." I make a nervous attempt to straighten the magazines on the coffee table and clear the three half-empty mugs from its surface. From the kitchen I call to Austin, a shabby semblance of bravado: "You want a beer?"

The phone answers me, four elongated siren calls before I find the courage to pick it up.

"Hello?"

"Is this Dolores Meredith?" Dr. Hindari's voice.

"Yes. You have the—"

"Negative. Of course the window . . ."

Negative. The virus doesn't show in my blood. The condoms. The odds. Luck. Fate. Backward blessings.

I feel Austin behind me. Dr. Hindari's heavy, melodious voice wafts from the receiver.

I shake my head no. Like a bullet comprehension hits me, deflected by the rush of self-preservation but in the end finding the bull's eye of sorrow that has been shrouded by my fear: Austin has HIV. Austin is going to die of AIDS. I am going to lose what I most love—and there is nothing I can do.

Austin's eyes well.

So many tears for so many reasons: fear, anger, grief, gratitude . . . love. Love is what his tears are for. For me. That I will not die even though he—

When all that you love is at once the source of your heart's greatest anguish, when you foresee that the practice of love in the moment will only make the withdrawal from love in the future more agonizing, you are faced with this choice: a single suffering, one moment of resolution, a decisive amputation. Or days and months and years of little losses, when the future wanes imperceptibly and sorrow chaperones you to heartbreak in small degrees.

I must choose.

I will allow myself this last embrace, I promise, as our arms encircle each other. For one last clasp, breast to breast, heart against heart, we hold our missing halves, our perfect selves, and keep disease at bay. For one last minute, only our breath and our bodies and our love exist.

This I will allow myself.

Then I will choose.

CHAPTER TWELVE

I cannot live with you —

❧

I cannot live with You—
It would be Life—
And Life is over there—
Behind the Shelf

The Sexton keeps the Key to—
Putting up
Our Life—His Porcelain—
Like a Cup—

Discarded of the Housewife—
Quaint—or Broke—
A newer Sevres pleases—
Old Ones crack—

I could not die—with You—
For One must wait
To shut the Other's Gaze down—
You—could not—

And I—Could I stand by—
And see You—freeze—
Without my Right of Frost—
Death's privilege?

Nor could I rise—with You—
Because Your Face—
Would put out Jesus'—
That New Grace

Grown plain—and foreign
On my homesick Eye—
Except that You than He
Shone closer by—

They'd judge Us—How—
For You—served Heaven—You know,
Or sought to—
I could not—

Because You saturated Sight—
And I had no more Eyes
For sordid excellence
As Paradise

And were You lost, I would be—
Though My Name
Rang Loudest
On the Heavenly fame—

And were You—saved—
And I—condemned to be—
Where You were not—
That self—were Hell to Me—

So We must meet apart—
You there—I—here—
With just the Door ajar
That Oceans are—and Prayer—
And that White Sustenance—
Despair—

EMILY DICKINSON 1862

SOMETIMES, IF I pause in the preparation of the next morning's lecture or sit too long in one room of my house, a seething anger takes hold of me, a flush of hot feeling so pure that I know if I were to touch my palm to the cold kindling on the andirons in the fireplace, it would ignite into blue flame.

Sometimes, if I forget to keep moving, one foot in front of the other in an absurd and endless field sobriety test, I am chilled to the bone with a despair so cruel that I know if I were to brush my hand or arm against another, it would crack from my body and fall to the ground like a porcelain icicle loosened from the limb of a winter cedar by an intruder.

Always, when my thoughts reach Dolores, I am seduced into a fever of hungers, cooled only when sleep sloughs off consciousness and desire is satisfied by dream.

Dr. Hindari has told me that I am in excellent condition, that with the administration of AZT and the habits of good health, it could be years before HIV turns AIDS. And I say to myself, after remarking to him his incredible, lopsided definition of "excellent," that I am not sure whether I want years.

What is time, I think, but the balancing act of love and pain. If pain outweighs love, what is time's worth, where lies its power of seduction?

It takes her over a week to find the courage to tell me.

It is a dismal Sunday morning, the dirty clouds behind the skeletal branches of the elms lifting just enough to cause hope of sunlight, then settling low again, an aching disappointment. I rake the wet leaves from the front garden, the long sweeps of the barbed teeth scoring the earth beneath. I am mindful of the withered remnants of the summer annuals; those that are yellowed and limp, I snip off at soil level, leaving the root balls to attempt the impossible: a second year of bloom. The tidied earth pleases me, so I stand with rake in hand and savor the only pleasure I've felt in weeks.

"Even in winter, it's lovely," she says, her voice behind me.

"You surprised me. . . . You're walking?"

"Yes. I felt like being out in this . . . this weather." She pushes through the gate. "The cleanup's coming along nicely. You forget the shape of these beds when they're in full flower." She bends to pick up a nasturtium kernel, which she juggles from fist to fist. I can see where the damp air has tamed the lively curls against the back of her neck.

"Will you come in? There's coffee on." I lean the rake against the porch railing.

"Coffee sounds good." Dolores kneels and presses the nasturtium seed into the smooth dirt at the base of the bald trumpet vine. "Probably won't germinate," she says, brushing her hands against her jeans. She follows me up the porch steps, through the front door, and into the kitchen, our movements stylized into a formal dance.

My back to her, I pull two mugs from the cupboard and pour coffee into them. Gripped by an insane superstition, I alternate pouring into each cup until the levels match exactly.

"Austin?"

I turn.

"I don't blame you."

I set the coffee in front of her. She marries her hands around the mug.

"This is something beyond anybody's guilt or responsibility or blame. I know that, and I don't—on any level—blame you." She sips the coffee and studies my face.

"So what I'm going to say, I want you to understand that it's not out of anger or—"

"You don't have to explain," I cut in.

"I *do* have to explain. I do."

"I know what you're going to say, Dolores. I know, believe me, I know. I might say it myself, if our positions were reversed." In the past week, with the image of Dolores flinching from my touch seared into my memory, I've asked myself one hundred times whether this is true, whether an afflicted man can appreciate the mortal recoil of skin from skin. Or whether I am barred from a convincing understanding because, strangely, for its victims this disease outlaws physical suspicion.

"You're trying to make it easier for me," she says, reading my thoughts. Tears spill from her eyes. "Can't you see that by making it easier you make it harder?"

She stands up awkwardly, knocking the table so coffee sloshes across the surface. Neither of us moves. I want to spare us both the pitiful disclosure designed to dispatch any future I might contrive, but I listen to Dolores's speech, the ingenuous confession she's prepared as my farewell.

"I wish that I could . . . stay with you through this . . . that I could keep up . . . keep you . . . through the—"

"Dolores, Dolores," I say, rising, wanting to wrap my arms around her shaking shoulders but knowing that the time for touch—reprieved for one undaunted minute in Dolores's kitchen twelve days ago—has passed.

"I wish that I were stronger than I am! It was all I could do . . . to come here today . . . I'm a quitter, Austin! I don't have the guts— I've never had the guts to live with . . . with wanting what I can't have . . . with losing something . . . every day, every hour . . . Don't you see?"

"I wouldn't ask it of you."

"I can't watch this happen, Austin. It makes me crazy with— I can't."

"I'll honor—"

"Please stop! Say what you're thinking! Or curse me!" Her fists are raised to her cheeks. "Hate me for being so selfish! I know what I am! But please, oh please, oh please don't be honorable. I couldn't bear, I can't—" She moves closer to me and raises her hand so I can feel its warmth graze my cheek, my statued countenance.

She can't put it into language. So I say it for her, my words the stricken match to a tinder of ungrounded hope, hope which survived unsuspected until this second. "Watch me flame out in the prime of life? Kick the old bucket? Pass away? Die from AIDS? Is that what you couldn't bear, Dolores?" The fevered match in my heart ignites, kindles. "Because that's what's going to happen, whether or not you stick around to watch."

Her weeping checked by my fierce tirade—perhaps I've given her what she needs, an antidote to the sympathy obligated by love—Dolores moves to the entryway. As she pulls open the front door and a bolt of cold air swirls into the house, she says, so faintly I may be imagining it: "Don't you see? I could do it if I didn't love you . . . I could do it if I didn't love you so much."

The door swings shut behind her. I fix on the unmatched pane, the asymmetry of the square of dull light, and I plummet into the remainder of my life, a freefall from grace.

I choose treatment with Dr. Hindari rather than with the clinic in Sacramento. When the time comes, he says, his hands resting on his portly belly as if we are two old friends sharing a snifter of brandy in his sitting room, of course I will need the expertise of the specialists. But until then, as long as he monitors the CD4 and T-cell counts and I am faithful to the medications, he agrees that the clinic isn't necessary. What about the rest of my life? he asks.

"Work?"

"Work, yes, that."

"Didn't even raise an eyebrow. I'm lucky to have a liberal employer, I guess. I told my dean before the insurers could, and for him, it appeared to be a nonissue. It seems to me"—I pause and breathe in—"that it will remain my private business until I choose otherwise."

"I would agree so." The thick lenses of his glasses reflect the fluorescent light from the bulb overhead, giving him a white-eyed omniscience. "And your girlfriend, Ms. Meredith?"

A portrait threatens—only the discipline of desperation has voided it from consciousness—a picture burgeoning into coherence: Dolores, her fog-damped curls close about her face, the love of my life confessing her fear.

I shake my head.

"You read the pamphlets I gave you last week?" For a man of medicine, his expressiveness is quaintly curtailed on the subject of sex, even though in the popular mind this disease of mine reeks of sex: the illicit serial gropings in dirty one-room walk-ups, the prodigal promiscuity beneath blinking neon, the drug-induced mating of red-eyed demons. He gestures behind his desk to the wall-to-wall bookcases, then inclines his head like a patient schoolmaster.

"Life goes on, Austin," he says, a generous Buddha. "Loving is a part of that. When she clears the window, you'll see."

We speak in code on the matter of Dolores's tests, Dr. Hindari and I. "No news," he will say lightly to flag each negative result without literally violating the confidentiality required of him. For five more months, at least, here in this clinic, our lives will intersect while we each trade blood for time. Some profound wisdom too deep for language ensures Dolores's health to me, just as an uncanny cellular cognition denied doubt of the HIV positive results yielded by my own blood. Then, my heart recognized as genuine the fatal conclusion of my own testing; now, that trained heart would speak if Dolores were threatened. My pulse would quicken, my nerves would blister—but she is safe, still.

The weeks pass. The semester's close grows near. The leaf-fall ends; the gardens of the Leland House are pristine, combed clean. Over Thanksgiving, I snowshoe in to Eagle Lakes, then spend the night in Truckee. On a Monday morning in early December, I get a call from Jack Mariani. He is going to be in San Francisco for the next week; can we meet for dinner? It will be a tonic for me, I tell him, to visit and to talk.

On a Saturday night, we meet in the lobby of the Fairmont. Jack has lost weight, but he seems to move slowly, as though the weight loss has made him heavier somehow, or as if the grinding wheels of age are running him down to an emaciation which will end in vapor, in a thin twist of vanishing fog. I am reading my own premature mortality into my good friend's alteration, I chide myself when his solid handshake pulls me against him for a welcoming hug, and I resolve to play the Austin Barclay Jack knew before I left New York.

When the waiter has arranged us at our table and a gentle symphony supplies the backdrop, I ask after Clair.

Jack fingers his knife. "We're living apart these days. Since October."

"I'm sorry to hear that, Jack." My words are the standard reading from Emily Post: a quickly murmured apology to signal the dismissal of the topic because any other response would establish a willingness to listen. Yet when Jack goes on to account for the separation, I feel a sincere sorrow that I would never have foreseen.

"Clair and I, we've always had what one might label an uneasy match," he says ruefully. "Early in the marriage, she had the children and I had work. In the overlap, when we did have time together, well, I guess I just kept my mouth shut and looked the other way. The coward's path."

Jack pauses while a white-shirted waiter bustles over our table, pouring water into the fluted goblets, his dark hands a practiced charade of solicitude.

"In retrospect I can see that I was putting up, putting off, because it was easier than rocking the boat. I always had a case in court and one of the kids was playing Hamlet or giving a piano recital, and it was easier—believe it or not—to let the discord slip by for the sake of this client or that child."

He raises his water to his lips, then forgets to drink and puts the water down, untouched.

"I began looking forward to retirement . . . to what that would mean for Clair and me, all that unblocked time . . ."

The waiter returns and tips the label of the Sauvignon toward Jack, who nods, then waves away the proffered tasting.

"Let me give you some advice, Austin. When you reach my age"—he chuckles at himself—"don't let yourself look back and say, 'Good Lord, how I've squandered my aptitude for loving a woman.' Don't let that happen, son."

I shift in my seat.

"You were right to leave New York, to make room in your days for more than the law."

Salad arrives, artfully tendered plates of butter lettuce and artichoke over which the dark hands grind pungent crumbs of black pepper. My hands flutter a napkin open and rest against my tensed thighs.

"Enough Ann Landers," he laughs, eyeing the salad. "You know what you're doing." He takes a mouthful of salad. "Listen to this godawful dietary regimen I've sworn to . . ."

Our talk turns to the firm, the stable of New York attorneys we know in common, the reigning champion at the racquetball club. After Jack's comedic monologue over whether or not to have dessert, when the dining room is empty except for a gaggle of teenagers supping in prom night splendor, we stand and shake hands, sealing a vow that he'll return to California the following summer, when I will give him what he calls the geriatric tour of my Sierras.

As I cross the dark bay with the city's skyline behind me and the blood red taillights caravanning across the bridge in front of me, I ask myself whether I know what I'm doing, the statement Jack put to me without realizing its jarring resonance. We can only know what we want, I decide, as the caged trusses of the bridge flash by, so does wanting the unrecoverable invalidate for us whatever knowledge we claim for ourselves? Does Jack, forty years into an inert marriage, allow himself to want otherwise? And does the knowledge that it can't be, that what's done is done, translate into regret?

Regret sickens me, the cloying self-referential dead end that spells the abolition of pleasure. I have been steeped in regret ever since my lunatic ascent up the walls of Yosemite. It was regret clothed in the wolf's hide of anger that made me lash out at Dolores, a shameful remembrance on which I won't let myself dwell. It's time to move on. My thoughts rise to the barren shale ridges of Donner Pass, their moonscape beauty. To Jason Loman's eager face framed by my office door. To the bud swells on the limbs of the Tryon Street trees. To my friendships with Jack and with Dr. Hindari, an Indian holy man holding temple in the dubious shrine of the Davis Medical Corporation.

To the attainment of the realization, advancing slowly but at last arrived, that I will not die with Jack's regret: that my heart knows what it means to love the woman who makes it whole with all its might, however briefly.

Early Sunday morning, I shoulder the old dresser in my bedroom and haul it down to the wood shop, where I lather it with stripping formula and scrape the peeling surface smooth. I sand the wood surfaces and pass the tips of my fingernails across the even drawer faces, another pleasure found. In the afternoon, when a steady rain pelts the house, I review the outline of the suit I've filed on behalf of the Yuba County UFW asking for reclamation of the year-round housing privileges granted by contract to field workers three years ago. When the two largest growers in the county deny winter-month housing to their field labor, in effect they exclude the children—citizens by birth most of them—from access to continuous schooling. The case looks good to me, the argument judicious. With the east-driven rain tapping against the panes of my bedroom window, I fall into a deep sleep, a sleep that leaves no memories for morning.

For the next week until the Christmas break, I am swamped by computer-generated final exams, the lengthy responses to my carefully worded essay questions.

"Professor Sampson always used scantron," Annie suggests to me from my door late one afternoon, her coat and umbrella holstered under her arm.

"Thanks for the tip, Annie." I smile at her. Professor Sampson has also left behind a scurrilous reputation in the corridors of King Hall, something I don't plan on doing. I listen to Annie's footsteps fade and return to my papers.

The day has grown night by the time I finish entering the grades, the computer screen in my darkened office the light by which I work. The ghost of Professor Sampson haunts me: the joke become part of the law school's oral tradition is that he retired ten years before he stopped teaching. Jack's mention of retirement set me thinking, made me realize that I will need to plot a retirement of a different kind. I will elect to step down from the podium before I leave a legacy of ineptitude behind me. I decide, with a sane resolve so determined that it lifts a veil of dread, that I will elect to step down from life the same way—before the inevitable disability that would leave me bedridden, hollow of any sensation except the perception of pain. For the first time in my life I can regard my father's death with unselfish appreciation. Rather than linger over what its too soon timing robbed from me, I see what my father was saved from, instead: the truncated delights, the circumscribed contentments, the amputated joys which are the prescription of terminal disease.

I should tell Dr. Hindari, it occurs to me, about this saving epiphany, except that he would remind me of my obligations to the present and censor my preoccupations with the future. Live, Austin, live, he would chant, and tell me, as he did last week, "You're not ill until you're ill." I would like to describe it to Dolores, this newborn peace, except that she, too, has censored me—from speech, from contact, from the atonement of love. The blank screen in front of me beckons, a silent conspirator to expression. Tell me, the screen offers. I tap out three lines, the keys at my fingertips the umbilicus to my soul, and a poem grows. Two hours later in the absolute and abandoned tranquility of King Hall, I lift the page from Annie's laser printer and fold it lengthwise. Writing these lines is enough, the catharsis complete. I fold the paper over again, a square of serenity, and tuck it into my suit pocket.

It is nearly ten when I reach the outskirts of Woodland. On the edge of town, almost beneath the freeway overpass, the neon script of the Xochimilco Cafe reminds me that I've not eaten since morning. Somebody—was it Rick Day?—swore there wasn't better Mexican food to be had in the entire valley, so despite the forbidding, shabby facade, I swing the Jeep into the litter-strewn lot and lock it up. If Woodland can be said to have a bad part of town, this is it. With the low refrain of the cars overhead and the lively strains of mariachi rising into the damp, dark air, I feel I am traversing twilight territory, where the blurred distinctions between should and should not invite transgression.

As if my jacket is an embarrassment to the cafe, a small waitress with an Indian face steers me quickly down the long, narrow bar. She settles me in the back at a red Formica table barely large enough to hold the bowl of green chili salsa and basket of chips which she slides wordlessly off her tray along with the laminated menu. The jukebox reverses from Spanish to English, from sweet entreaties for *mi amor* to yodeled invective against the gal who got my pickup, shotgun, and dawg. Biculturalism in action, I muse, as I dip a corn chip into the salsa and pray that my beer comes quick.

The tortillas are handmade, the rice smells of cumin and fresh cilantro. The little waitress serves me without a word, then leaves my table to seat a couple who follow her into a booth across the room, beneath the single window of the Xochimilco where the neon CAFE sign backlights their heads, turning them to shadow puppets. She returns with a platter of picadillo and beans and points to my beer.

"*Sí, gracias,*" I say and watch her work her way to the crowded bar.

In one of those suddenly hexed moments when raucous sound descends to zero, when a room filled with catcall and clinking and melody hushes, a single word is spoken, usurping center stage.

"Henry."

Then the sound resumes: a drinker at the bar sets his shot glass down, hard; the jukebox record leads off with Spanish too rapid-fire for translation; in the kitchen, someone drops a pan and swears, a bilingual patois of oaths.

I recognize her voice.

I recognize the haloed outline of her hair, the quick flight of her hands.

And though I've never seen Henry Talmouth in the flesh, I recognize his shadowed self, too, from Dolores's description of the man she'd chosen who, being wrong in every way, could never disappoint her, could never bring her to the chaos of despair by way of desire.

Henry Talmouth.

The heart's prophylactic.

From my dark seat—the vantage point of an ambusher—I survey the pantomime of their dialogue. Henry talks, Dolores nods. Henry sips from a long-necked bottle, Dolores pushes her hair from her face. Henry reaches a hand to touch Dolores's wrist, Dolores tips the hand from her wrist and lifts her glass. The waitress stops at their booth, exchanges words with Dolores, who reaches her palm to the small woman's shoulder and rests it there in the unreserved touch of an old friend.

I shuffle bills from my wallet and tuck them halfway beneath the cold platter of picadillo. The small man stirring beef in the kitchen looks up, surprised, when I push through the swinging door. He could be, probably is, the Indian twin to the waitress who served me so efficiently, who conserved conversation for the *rubia*.

"Yeah," he says when I point to the door, cracked open to chill the heat generated by the crackling grill in the tiny kitchen.

At home, upstairs in my bedroom, I too chill the room with an open window, letting the night wind cape me as I lie on my bed. If I can lower the temperature of my soul enough, if I can lure the mercury of my thought below freezing, to the temperature of forgiveness, I will be able to find sleep, death's second self.

It encroaches in minuscule movements, forgiveness, but in the predawn torment of the insomniac I've achieved it: the erasure of jealousy, the cancellation of bitterness.

I fall asleep with skin as cold as ice, with blood frozen and breath so dull it could escape a mirror's reflection.

What a fine spirit I've designed for myself.

What a resiliency the gallowed man assumes.

What a lesson to buy my soul's freedom from the karmic chains.

What Dolores must feel.

CHAPTER THIRTEEN

The soul has bandaged moments —

The Soul has Bandaged moments—
When too appalled to stir—
She feels some ghastly Fright come up
And stop to look at her—

Salute her—with long fingers—
Caress her freezing hair—
Sip, Goblin, from the very lips
The Lover—hovered—o'er—
Unworthy, that a thought so mean
Accost a Theme—so—fair—

The soul has moments of Escape—
When bursting all the doors—
She dances like a Bomb, abroad,
And swings upon the Hours,

As do the Bee—delirious borne—
Long Dungeoned from his Rose—
Touch Liberty—then know no more,
But Noon, and Paradise—

The Soul's retaken moments—
When, Felon led along,
With shackles on the plumed feet,
And staples, in the Song,

The Horror welcomes her, again,
These, are not brayed of Tongue—

EMILY DICKINSON 1862

"PEOPLE DON'T BUY houses in January, anyway," says Zoey, setting a cup of jet black coffee in front of me on the jumbled desk.

"So? When have we ever shut down in January?"

"I'm not talking about shutting down the office, Dolores. I'm talking about you taking some time off—"

"You think I'm incapable of doing a job I've done for twenty years?" The coffee burns my tongue, its potent bitterness a reprimand to the wicked temper I have shown my dearest friend.

"Of course not. But—"

"But what? Spit it out."

"But you're not yourself . . ."

I let the caesura lengthen, a sustained minor chord, before I answer.

"You really want to ask how in the world I could have seen Henry again, don't you? You want to insinuate your prissy morality into my life and pass your priggish naive blanket judgments on my behavior, don't you?"

My words are a bomb to which Zoey has held a match, the candled wick flaming to explosion point.

"Look," she tries again. "I don't know what happened between you and Austin—"

"You're absolutely right!" I am standing now, knowing I don't want to hurt her with these choked cruelties even as they are crawling off my tongue, that I will regret and repent and sorrow over these words as I have over so many that I've spoken in the past month. But once the gate valve is open, they spill out, the poisoned torrents of stifled emotions, suspect self-pity diverted into aggression.

I bend over and thrust my face into hers. "You know nothing, less than nothing. You know bullshit about what's happening to me!" My fists clench, my face swells to a wrathful tint. "Bullshit! Nothing!"

Zoey stares at me, a polar mask.

I grab my bag, but it catches on the arm of the swivel chair behind my desk. I yank the bag free; the chair tumbles sideways to the floor.

"Sell the goddamn place for all I care," I say, one foolish parting abuse, and trip over my own feet on my way out the door.

If only I could cry, I wish to myself when I still my trembling hands against the frigid steering wheel of the Volvo, if only tears would come and the venom inside me would evaporate into grief. If only. If only. The Volvo's engine won't crank, so I leave the car and walk, heedless of either direction or destination. Once, looking up, I find myself in the lot of a Jiffy Mart. My bare hands have stiffened in the cold wind, so I push through the heavy glass door and stand inside, my fingers pressed into my armpits. I stand there for so long that the teenaged clerk behind the register turns from his television screen and stares, a bold challenge. I fumble open my wallet, find money, pay for a bottle of port, and wrestle it into my bag instead of accepting the sack the clerk offers.

I am so cold when I reach the apartment that the key slips from my hand, and it is two tries before the lock unlatches and I swing the door open. Milton looks up from sleep, winks at me, and nestles his head against the afghan.

In the bathroom I shed my clothes and run a tub of scalding water. I rinse the ceramic cup holding my toothbrush and unscrew the port, filling the cup to the brim. The bathwater makes me ache when I lower myself into it, the burn sliding up my skin. I sink into the water to my neck, rest my head against the rim, and swallow from the cup: one, two, three gagging gulps of the sour wine.

In two weeks, I have botched as many sales, easy sales, the kind every realtor looks forward to: qualified buyers and eager sellers. I lost the Munsons yesterday, the first time in my career to forfeit clients, after showing them a ninth house and then losing patience, evicting the sweat-suited couple from the Buick.

"Try Century 21," I told them through the cracked window. "Maybe someone there can decipher your demands. I certainly can't."

I can't decipher myself, either, as the bathwater cools around me and a headache blooms behind my eyes. I have tried to make business the salve it has been in the past: the columns of numbers and the prorations, the clauses and the inspections, the done deals. But the human element—the frowzy housewives and the heel-worn husbands, the barking kids who want the kidney-shaped pool with the tiled seahorses—I can't cope anymore, can't adapt myself to their predictable fits and starts, can't bear to abet their fatuous preferences. Even Zoey (whom I love, I do love Zoey) sets me on edge with her patterned dogmas, the practice of tolerance and composure and forbearance, all of them disguises fencing real feeling. My impatience is unfair, I know, yet the human circus evokes from me distaste bordering loathing, the invidious detritus of fortune's disfavor.

When Mrs. Margaret Munson, wife to Floyd, shook her head at the pretty flower beds behind house number three—"Too much weeding"—I recoiled from the picture of Austin's strong hands setting the delphinium into the earth of the Leland House gardens, our future laid out in the delicate sprays of green. When Mr. Floyd Munson, father to screeching Suzanne and black-hearted Patrick, slammed the front door of house number seven—"Something's not even"—I flinched at the memory of Austin's patient perfectionism in squaring the porch, the pleasure on his face when the bubbles of his level floated center in the wooden windows showing the corrected cant. Every new encounter wounds me with old recollection, and the recollection pierces me with fresh anguish.

Standing at arm's reach from Austin in the kitchen of the Leland House three months ago, abetted by my greatest strength, I made the choice I have always made: to turn heel and walk away from further damage. Yet I didn't walk; I ran. In the aftermath of my crazed flight to self-preservation, in the cooldown of a calmed pulse, I see what I've run toward is not a placid expanse of sternly stifled regret, but instead a terrain treacherous with memorials to a happiness I will never find again.

I thought I could make myself stop thinking of Austin.

I can't.

I am sabotaged by memories: his boyish captivation with everyday miracles, his yearning hands against my skin . . . his faith in me . . . in what I was. Love remembered intrudes itself, carving an aching hollow inside me that refuses to be solaced by the frauds I scheme.

The bathwater is tepid, the port half-empty, when a rude banging on the apartment door stirs me to rise from the bath. I don't bother to turban my dripping hair or blot the water from my skin. I tug the robe hanging from the makeshift plastic hook on the bathroom wall and the plastic breaks, dropping the robe to the water-soaked floor.

"Shit," I say, stooping, and rise to face Henry Talmouth.

"Make yourself at home," I tell him, pushing past him into my bedroom and fishing a T-shirt from the pile of clothes at the end of my bed.

"Dolores," he says in his Henry-being-reasonable voice, his ringed hand straightening an imagined wisp of his thinning hair. "You weren't answering the door, and the door was not locked."

Milton lands on the clothes and sits, his tail twitching.

"I wasn't answering the door because I was in the bath, as should be apparent."

"Did you forget our date?"

"Henry," I say, sitting on the bed to pull on a pair of jeans, "we have never in seven and a half years had a *date.*"

"We said Zeke's at three? Didn't you remember?" He sits beside me, eyeing the laundry pile, half of which I've dumped to the floor at my feet. "*I* did."

"Good for you, Hen. I must have forgotten." I tuck my T-shirt in, zip my pants, and dig through the clothes for my Garfield socks.

"Are you drunk, Dolores?"

"Half a bottle of port—not one of your favorites, Henry, so I won't offer you a glass."

Henry makes me sick.

I make myself sick.

"Dolores," he says, "I came here because I need to tell you something."

He stands and moves to my dresser, where he picks up Jorge's hammer head and sets it down, brushing his hands together like a nervous fly.

"Tell away," I say, the wine a creeping nausea in my throat.

"When we started again, it wasn't the same, was it?" Henry is earnest, absolutely serious. His emotional sensors are working overtime: something, he's detected, is not right with this affair.

I let him go on.

"When you broke it off, I thought you'd come around eventually. And you did, Dolores. And then when I saw you in town, I was really glad to be with you again."

I pet Milton with my orange foot.

"But it's not . . . fun, anymore. Not like it used to be. So,"— his conclusion rushes out—"I think we should end it. Now. Today."

I could teach Henry what it means to end something, that something never rightly begun has no potential for ending, that endings are about what matters, what's dear to us beyond belief. That when we end what matters, when we sever the love that makes us whole and right with the world, long, ghastly fingers reach into our souls and steal them away so we are left to walk about like zombies.

But Henry wouldn't understand, and I don't want him to.

I stand, a little tippy, and slap my palms against my hips.

"You're absolutely right," I tell him, extending my hand for a shake. "Let's call this quits."

Henry can understand this, a contract sealed man-to-man. He shakes my hand and backs out of the apartment, relief inflating his features.

I am going to be sick. Not because of Henry—a double-made mistake than I would have corrected, finally, had he not—but because the thick wine and the dirty clothes and the empty apartment and the shame that rises like bile in my gorge are what are left me now.

Still, I cannot cry.

I hang my head over the toilet and retch. Milton sits on the bath mat and watches, his head frozen in curiosity. I rinse my mouth with water—the cup tasting faintly of port—and lay my face down on the cold floor.

Hours later, into the evening, Zoey wakes me with a cool washcloth against my forehead.

"You've been sick," she says, straightening the pillowcase under my head. "Can you sit up to drink?" She lifts a steaming cup from the bedside table.

I nod and winch myself slowly upright. "How did I get into bed?"

"Ted. It scared me when you left the Volvo."

"It wouldn't start. I walked."

"Ted says it was the battery cable. He brought it home. We found you in there." She nods to the bathroom and doesn't, thankfully, say what else she found.

"You're burning up, Dolores," she says, slipping the washcloth back against my hair. "Can you drink this?"

"What is it?"

"It's just soup . . . it won't kill you. Here's Tylenol and water. I would guess you haven't eaten—"

"Oh, Milton, either. Will you—?"

"I already have. He's outside now." Zoey begins sorting the clothes on the bed and the floor, making neat piles of whites and coloreds, heavy and light. "I'm going to start a load. I'll be right back."

I hold the cup against my cheek, then sip the broth. Zoey returns to the bedside.

"If you can sit up, I'll change these sheets," she says.

"I'm sorry for what I said, Zoe."

"It's done," she says, shaking her head. "You didn't mean it."

"I *didn't* mean it. I would never in my right mind say—"

She looks at me, eyebrows raised.

I go on. "I'm not myself, you said it yourself. I've been—"

"You don't need to tell me. You didn't want to talk about it, and you don't have to now."

"It's not Henry. That's over, anyway. Henry was a relapse . . .

a painkiller . . . a fix. I know it was pointless. It will never happen again, believe me."

She waits, good Zoey, practicing patience.

When I'm settled on the couch in clean pajamas and the twin motors of the washer and dryer make the apartment homey, as if a sane and responsible person lives here, I see that Zoey has vacuumed the living room, carted the random dirty dishes into the kitchen, shelved my strewn books, picked up my mail from beneath the drop.

She bustles around the kitchen and pauses to call out to me, "Jorge called. Several times."

She comes into the living room with a tray of cheese sandwiches, which she settles on the coffee table in front of me.

"Eat," she says, and takes a sandwich herself. "Coffee?"

"Maybe juice? I think there's orange left in the fridge."

When the sandwiches are eaten and Zoey is loading our plates into the dishwasher, I call to her.

"Zoe? Come here, please."

She sits on the couch next to me, a dishcloth in her hands.

"I am going to take time off . . . if you're willing . . ."

"I can handle the office, Dolores. It's not as if they're knocking down our doors."

"I messed up with the Munsons, I know."

"Look," she says, folding the cloth into a tidy square, "let's just say you're taking a long-deserved vacation. It would be true, and that's that. No further explanation is required."

I want to tell her. I want her to know that even though I may have seemed to be sailing off the deep end, there was a reason. And I want to hear myself tell this narrative, to make certain I got the story right. So I take her hand and walk her through Austin's diagnosis; his escape to Yosemite; the dripping porch of the Leland House and the boundless, reverberating moment he spoke the words HIV positive; Dr. Hindari and the retesting; my decision to turn away . . . the resumption of indifference with Henry. When I have no more to tell, when the words run out and I am left with an ache in my chest that has become as familiar to me as my heart-beat, I don't know anymore where the story ends. Zoey is crying when I finish, quiet tears she doesn't wipe away because both of her hands are clasping mine, two sets of palms pressed together in the tight clench of blood brothers.

Some say sympathy doesn't heal, that the walking wounded are reduced by sympathy, belittled by its inherent falsity; how can the sympathizer fathom the full horror, after all, of a tale such as Austin's and mine. But what I find when I've exhausted myself with the telling and my best friend lets her tears fall unchecked is that Zoey's sympathy thaws the icy bars around my heart.

Curled against her breast, cradled in her arms, I can cry. At last, in a grieving long refused by the wrong kind of passion, I weep. My mourning is for Austin's loss and mine, for the loss of the rare and magical thing we'd made between us, the entire people we became when our selves joined. I find myself crying for Austin alone, for the absent liberties which the long-lived take for granted, seldom grateful for their daily gifts. For the decline into death that AIDS dictates. I cry for myself, that the choice I've made has failed to divorce me from either this constant sense of profligate waste or its faithful companion, the inevitable prospect of final sorrow. Sorrow will be mine forever, whether Austin and I are separated by twelve blocks or twelve thousand miles, were I to see him daily or never again. And waste—Smart Dolores! The canny woman of the business world! The queen of the profit motive! I thought I could turn this into a break-even deal: what I can't have, I will refuse to let myself want.

But the figures in my heart don't tally.

Zoey strokes my hair, cups my cheek with her palm. "I'm not going to ask you if you feel better now, Dolo," she whispers.

"Oh, Zoey." I sit up straight on the couch. "I'm so good at not feeling I don't know what I do feel . . . But I'll *be* better, I promise."

Zoey squeezes my hand. "I'm going to move the wash," she says, rising from the couch.

She brings a basket of dry clothes into the living room. We sit on the couch sorting and folding in silence. When the piles sit neatly on the coffee table, we decide that I will take two, even three weeks off. Zoey will let me know if something extraordinary requires me back at the office; I will give her my itinerary if I decide to leave Woodland for long.

When Ted's honking calls her from my living room, she lays her hand on my shoulder.

"Thank you, Zoey. For this and more than this." I wave my hand at the neatened room.

She kisses my cheek. "I told Jorge you would see him."

I nod to her yes, I will see Jorge.

I wake early the next morning, Milton soft against my chest. The sky is overcast and bleak; rain would be better, I think when I let Milton slip through the back door and pick his way across the damp concrete of the patio. Rain would be action, movement, a cleansing passage into the next season, a cancellation of winter's melancholy inertia. I shower and hang my towels up neatly, tuck my pajamas into the empty hamper. The piles of laundered clothes in my bedroom are emblems of Zoey's faith that I will get on with it, that my wallowing is through. I pull on jeans and a heavy sweater and make coffee in the kitchen, first settling Milton's filled dish on the floor. When the coffee drains, Milton paws the kitchen door. I let him inside, and he walks across the kitchen floor to look into his dish. He crosses to sit at my feet, then leaps into my lap and settles in, purring.

"Not hungry, Milts?" I ask him, stroking his wide back, feeling the winter damp caught up in his fur.

Small children and animals, it is said, can read emotions when adult interpretations fail. Trust their instincts, folklore advises, and you will find your way to the truth. Milton is husbanding me, I realize, knowing that if he doesn't eat now, he can eat later, that I will take care of him after he takes care of me, when I no longer need him draped warmly across my legs, centering me like an anchor into this time and place.

In late morning I drive south of town to where Jorge and

Julian live in the labor shacks on Bianchi Road. Jorge should be in school on a Wednesday, but often he isn't, I know from past experience: the many telephone calls placed to my office throughout the workday hours a giveaway that he's missed the bus or feigned sickness rather than attend school. Arinda Mesa says absenteeism is typical when farm families stay less than a year in one district. I think Jorge's attendance problems are a consequence of his living in a house with too many adults and too many worries, with too little space and too little childhood.

The Volvo bumps over the rutted, muddied road in front of the line of narrow shacks. If the engine breaks down or the chassis sinks into mud, I'll just walk away from it, I swear to myself, and whoever wants it can dig it out and drive it off. Jorge's house is the last in the line, where the bare fields take over and the clotted earth spreads for flat acre after flat acre. I leap from the car to the cement stoop over a pothole the size of a small bathtub and knock on the hollow door. Still echoing my last knock, the door opens and Jorge flies into my arms.

"Hello, kiddo," I say, hugging his wiry body and smelling him: the scent of little boy dirt and onions and turned cooking oil. "Do you want to come out and eat with me? To McDonald's, maybe?"

He nods yes, all bright brown eyes and solemnity.

"We need to leave a note for your papa, okay? Here, you help me write it." Jorge prints the words, asking me for spellings as he writes, and I decide that I will run by his school with him to see the principal and to devise a plan that will ensure he's in class with the other children where he should be, instead of alone in the drafty shack. I need to establish myself as some kind of legitimate part-time guardian, Arinda said, translating my words into Spanish for Julian, if I want to become a support system for Jorge. I make sure that Jorge writes "DOLORES" in square letters at the bottom of the page, so that even if Julian doesn't understand our primer English, he will know Jorge is with me.

In McDonald's, with Jorge painting french fries into ketchup the color of Hollywood blood across the waxed sheet of paper that jacketed his cheeseburger, I consider how inconsequential one little dark-skinned boy is to the teacher who'd assumed he'd moved away; to the principal who has neither time, money, nor inclination for truant checks; to the district entrusted with Jorge's education. I remember an activist rallying cry, one I'd then chosen to ignore, from my aesthetic tenure at Cal: when institutions fail, individuals can't. I will talk with Arinda about the sponsorship she mentioned, the CASA program in which unrelated adults can become protectors to children like Jorge, aunts and uncles by conscious consideration rather than blood.

I leave Jorge on the cement stoop of his house, the McDonald's sack holding Julian's hamburger a flag in his raised hand. (Jorge's idea—"Papa too," he said when we stood at the counter and watched the costumed girl's fingers press the pictographs. "Because she can't read as well as you," I told him, serious, and then told myself that I would get him a storybook, something without rhyme, at Eddie's on the way home.) As the Volvo shudders its way over the muddy tracks, I recognize that for two hours I have lifted out of myself, out of the lethargic drag that seemed to have stolen my soul. I can do this for Jorge, I tell myself, I can move into his life and it will matter, my guardian presence and generous motives propelling him into a long future: into adulthood and beyond, onward to old age and a kindly timed death.

A kindly timed death. In the end, I always return to Austin. What is happening to Austin has flattened the contours of event and episode so that no matter where I am, in the deconstruction of despair or the manufacture of purpose, the subdued landscape of my life is an amphitheater from which, having refused a front row seat, I can only wonder what might be playing now had I written the story differently. So abruptly that I pop the clutch and stall the Volvo at the stop sign on the highway, I realize my wonder has converted to need: I *need* to know. I need to know how his days are passed: what he's writing on the computer screen in his office at King Hall, whether Jason Loman makes him laugh today, how he falls asleep at night—his hand outstretched or curled under his chin. I need to know because those brief banked months of memories we've made are not enough to satisfy the urgent greediness that clamors inside my head, rotating me from past to present like the cosmos spinning the earth from night into day.

I told Zoey I don't know what I feel. But this I recognize.

Eddie's is nearly empty. With the holidays over, book selling slows, he tells me, pulling his graying hair into a rubber band, and steers me to the coffee pot wafting French roast into the warm air of his shop.

"Houses, too," I say, and pour myself a cup.

Eddie runs the perfect bookstore. He doesn't broadcast his opinions, though he holds strong ones. His recommended reading list is always more considered than the best-sellers in the *Times*, his coffee the best you can buy in town, except that at Eddie's coffee is free. He will continue to shelve books from his personal good list long after they've been remaindered at B. Dalton's, and he refuses ever to stock the kind of paperbacks that fill the check-out racks at Lucky's. If you browse for an hour without buying a book, Eddie will come around and refill your cup, straighten a few crooked volumes on one of the narrow, tightly ordered shelves, then go back to his reading perch behind the maple counter. It's like visiting the library of an old friend, being in Eddie's, a friend with whom you can sit without the constraint of conversation.

On the children's shelf I find *Where the Wild Things Are* for Jorge and slide it under my arm. I follow the new fiction titles to poetry, slender paperback chapbooks where every line makes sense, where every word justifies its choice among all possible choices, earning a perfect placement in each broken line. I have two weeks off, I remind myself: two weeks without a calendar convenient to other people's lives, when I can measure the passage of time with pages instead of hours. I study the titles on the wall of literature at the end of Eddie's store, a dark tunnel housing whole worlds built on language. The warm coffee-scented air, the shadows between the tall shelving, the rustling pages of Eddie's book—all conspire to translate me to childhood, to Daddy's upstairs study, in a conflation of space and time that overtakes me so suddenly and with such force that I sink to the floor and sit cross-legged, trapped in the inversion of history.

I would time travel backward if I could, to the sweet safety of Daddy's lap and a good-night story where the resolution never failed to ease me into a trusting sleep, sure that the shackles on the vanquished monsters would hold, their tempered strength secured by my father's gentle, low-pitched voice. Jorge may have outgrown already that safety and the child's doctrine it underwrites: that if we do our part—sound out the words, a syllable at a time!—the fates will reward us with a happy ending. I open the Sendak book I have picked for him and read through it, tracking the changing expression on little Max's face as the wild things tempt and terrorize him. I come to these lines:

And when he came to the place where the wild things are
they roared their terrible roars and gnashed their terrible teeth
and rolled their terrible eyes and showed their terrible claws
till Max said "BE STILL!"
and tamed them with the magic trick—

and I am crying again, the tears I didn't finish crying yesterday, because I see no way to circumvent the felony committed against Austin's life, no cure by sentencing, no magic trick.

They must be Eddie's feet approaching, called to me by the lament I muffle against my sleeve. A hand touches my shoulder.

"Try this," the familiar voice says. "It might work."

I lift my head and see the hand—not Eddie's—its hearty grip encasing *The Complete Poems of Emily Dickinson*, the slender, strong fingers flexed around the thick volume.

I raise my eyes to Austin's face.

He bends down. Our faces are so close we could kiss if we were to choose.

"The Soul—" he begins, a fairy-tale opening.

"—has Bandaged moments," I close, a tragedy.

CHAPTER FOURTEEN

Title divine — is mine!

ॐ

Title divine—is mine!
The Wife—without the Sign!
Acute Degree—conferred on me—
Empress of Calvary!
Royal—all but the Crown!
Betrothed—without the swoon
God sends us Women—
When you—hold—Garnet to Garnet—
Gold—to Gold—
Born—Bridalled—Shrouded—
In a Day—
Tri Victory
"My Husband"—women say—
Stroking the Melody—
Is this—the way?

EMILY DICKINSON 1862

I SAW THE Jeep this morning, the back of his dark head, the curls at the nape of his neck touching the collar of his shirt. His shoulders were square, both steady hands on the wheel. Seeing him surprises my heart with—not joy, too shallow, that—but such a deep and pleasured satisfaction that throughout the morning meeting with our accountant and the preliminary paper thrashing with Zoey and the pretax calculations with the adding machine dangling its curly white tape like a ribboned roadway to redemption, I smile. Throughout the commonplace tasks I use to hold myself together,

I smile, such an aberration from what has become my holding pattern for hope that Zoey notices. The office feels strangely peaceful, an orderly oasis alphabetized and tallied, a placid bastion against the chaos of the universe. The accountant leaves holding the file folders which absolve my life from federal castigation or even official notice: Dolores Meredith, forty-one, never married, no dependents, supports herself and employs one, pays her taxes promptly, remembers to feed her cat.

I am more than that. I can be more.

"You must be feeling better," Zoey says. "Last year at tax time you threatened to take a Princess Cruise to Alaska until he finished . . . you remember?"

"God, yes, I remember."

I study the newly sharpened pencil in my hand, the sharp circular edge of the eraser's tip, the scalloped line between the orange paint and the wood grain, the lead dark core. Beginnings, fresh pencils have always meant to me. I remember the September refrain, the late-summer Saturday morning excursions to the downtown Woolworth's, Daddy's big hand enclosing my little one, the studied foray up and down the musky aisles, the search for the pencils and paper with which I would write out my new life in second or fifth or seventh grade. I insisted on carrying my paper kit of student tools because every half block or so as we walked to the Capitol I needed to peek inside and glimpse the cellophane-wrapped packets to verify that the slow clerk had bagged each precious buy. Later, with Todd and Daddy as my audience, I would open them at the kitchen table and array them in a formal place setting: pencils on the left, paper in the middle, pens on the right, a stack of rectangular rubber erasers in the corner where, in years to come, I would learn to put a wineglass.

We would buy sandwiches and Cokes from a vendor who was accustomed to selling lunch to the governor, Daddy said. On a shady bench on the Capitol lawn we spread our picnic. I can see the green bottles of Coke, the butcher-paper plates with the ham sandwiches and pickles. I can hear my father's consecration over our communion meal: the passionate lines from Christopher Marlowe and Robert Herrick and Andrew Marvell against the chorus of cars making the lunch rush down K Street. " 'The grave's a fine and private place,' " he would quote to me, leaning against the bench, a Coke in his hand. " 'But none, I think, do there embrace . . .' Think, now, Dolores, about what the poet's telling us." Early, too early for me to understand, he taught me the responsory: "Carpe diem, Daddy!" Then I would slide my new pencils from the bag and tell him all the stories I was ever going to write.

Carpe diem, my father taught me, so well that I never failed his quizzes.

Daddy's literary favorites were all buried by the eighteenth century, so Dickinson I found for myself in eleventh grade (I bought my pencils alone by then) in the pages of poetry Mrs. Antonini skipped in order to make time for our obligatory honors production of *Hedda Gabler*. The abrupt, cryptic lines entranced me; the recursive decoding of suffering a message I met with a recognition so acute it short-circuited the language lobe of my brain and settled straight into my heart. Yet I haven't read Dickinson in years, not until Austin handed me the complete poems in Eddie's. When I read from her now, a prayerful undertaking because *his* hands delivered the text, her verses draft for me a covenant, a vow that rends rapture from woe. I am filled with a robust tranquility, a fortitude that urges me forward: to salvage time, to seize these days.

"Dolores?"

"Sorry, Zoe." I shake my head, a quick flash-forward. "I was caught up in a time warp."

"I was thinking of you and Jorge . . . I clipped this, if you didn't see it, about the Children's Museum exhibit." Zoe sets the newsprint down on my desk. "In case you're running out of ideas . . ."

"Thanks." I scan the article, then fold it in quarters and file it into my bag. I let out a sigh, stretch my arms above my head, and swing my legs across the desktop. When Zoey is rinsing the coffee pot in the back room, I call out, "You know what I've found, Zoe?"

She turns off the tap. "Sorry—what did you say?"

"Do you know what seems to be most important to Jorge?" Zoey sits in one of my client chairs, positions it for a leisurely afterwork chat. "The trips and the clothes and the medical aren't as important as the security? It seems as long as Jorge knows I'm here, as long as he knows that if he needs me I'm around, the rest of the program is sort of secondary. Of course I know how important the eye checks and the teacher conferences and the library card are, but for him . . . for him the big thing is that I'm Dolores . . . that he can count on me."

Zoey is grinning at me. "It's amazing that you figured that out. For a woman without children, I mean . . . It makes you happy, sponsoring him, doesn't it?"

"It makes me happy . . . it makes me rich."

"You might not say that after Donald the wonder accountant crunches those numbers we saddled him with," she teases.

"I might not," I agree. "And then again, I might."

In April, I do take Jorge to the exhibit, where his face lights up with the proper wonder when he meets himself in holograph and mans the simulated spaceship through a planetarium galaxy. We buy Julian a balancing man built of bent iron spikes. He dances on the head of a twelve-penny nail like the ones Austin used to set the studs in the walls of the Leland House. He reminds me of myself: teetering back and forth to the pendulum of his outstretched arms, dipping and turning without slipping from his safe foothold. I can't resist walking Jorge across the Capitol lawns, where he trusts me to hold the balancing man and runs at the pigeons, disrupting their scavenging, sending them into momentary, meteoric flight.

It makes me rich to present Jorge with books, and Julian has built him a lone pine shelf on which he stockpiles his growing library. Our treat is to stop in at Eddie's after the poetry workshop when Jorge, seated in the beanbag chair in the children's aisle, performs a lengthy comparative analysis to determine the week's selection. Eddie knows Jorge by now—a steady customer, he calls him—and watches the trade magazines for Spanish-language chil-

dren's books that he casually shelves between the beginning read-
ers like Easter surprises.

"*Mira, Dolores, mira!*" Jorge exclaims when he finds Eddie's
gifts, delighted to become the possessor of the Spanish version of
the same book we picked last week.

He is engrossed with just such a find now, his face tilted so close
to the illustrated pages that I am tempted to doubt the optometrist's
clean bill of health. I lean against Eddie's counter and watch him
unbox the afternoon's UPS delivery, which he sets, one by one, face
up on the maple surface.

> *A Guide to HIV Care*
> *Caring for a Loved One with AIDS*
> *Anatomy of an Illness*
> *Mortal Embrace: Living with AIDS*
> *Alive and Well: A Path for Living in a Time of HIV*

Eddie looks up from the empty box. "No poetry today?"

"Today? No, just Jorge's—thanks, Eddie." My hand rests deliberately on the stack of books. I trace the words . . . *Alive and
Well*.

"Special order?" I say, breathing out.

"One's a request . . . a friend . . . I started looking through *Books
in Print* and thought I'd stock the others." Eddie laughs, a sad guf-
faw. "The world's not all lyric poetry these days, is it?" He lifts the
books and rests them against his hip, schoolboy style.

I hold Jorge extra long in front of his little house. He is im-
patient in my arms; he wants to run inside and compare his new
story with last week's. He can't wait to read the story in English to
Julian, who will follow along in the Spanish text, his field-worn
hands handling the pages as if they are sacred scrolls. *Living with
AIDS*, I hear the phrase inside my head when Jorge closes the door
behind him. *Alive and Well*, I see the bold script the size of mar-
quee letters when Jorge lifts the threadbare curtain and presses his
face against the cloudy window glass. *Mortal Embrace*, I say to my-

self when, the winter night falling, I pull up to the curb at the apartment: Dickinson could have titled it.

Except Dickinson never titled anything. Because a poem without a title escapes expectation, coaches you to discard preconception, invites you to figure it out, all by yourself. The way I am doing with Austin's life, and mine.

Early Saturday morning, I meet new clients at the office. The Howards want to escape Oakland, to sell out of the modest home in which they have lived for thirty-four years and put space around themselves. They want a place where Grandma and Grandpa can keep chickens and ducks and geese to show the grandchildren during summer vacations, to teach them firsthand about food chains and life cycles and the human responsibility for the earth's slowly diminishing carrying capacity. In flat midwestern tones Helen Howard explains that she has never ceased yearning for the animal seasons she grew up with on a family farm in Iowa, how for all the years she and Kent battled the East Bay freeways she was biding her time, building their savings, waiting to cup feeble golden hatchlings in her hands once again as she had done, a toddling child, outside Griswold. For the city grandchildren, she says to me, but it's her joy I imagine warming the incubating eggs, her hands scooping up the fragile fluffs of down and holding them to her cheek. I like Helen and Kent, the sensible flannels and old jeans they have worn for marching across the quicksand furrows of the rural properties I show them, the preference Kent confesses for sagging wooden outbuildings to aluminum pole barns.

They are taken by a three-acre parcel, the western edge bordered by a row of Valley oaks. When Kent has discovered the concrete stem-wall of the original farmhouse and Helen has figured that the natural depression beneath the oaks is deep enough for a pond, they turn to me and say yes, this is it, if they can sell the Oakland place.

"We'll work it out," I tell them, and we drive back to the office, calculating.

Lassitude overtakes me after I've set up a file for the Howards' offer. It's all I can do to load myself into the Volvo. The engine rolls, a low wah-wah-wah, and the car rests, dead. I don't have the strength to call the tow people, to sit on the pink vinyl chairs in the cigarette-staled waiting room of the garage while the mechanic calculates the damages and his Saturday wages. Instead, I trade keys and take the Buick, turn the efficient heater on high, and punch on the radio.

I'm not sure how I reach Eddie's, whether I take Second Street and then turn left on Main or follow High all the way to the intersection. In one of those psychic impasses where we lose minutes and consciousness, when we later look back, mystified, and ask ourselves who could have been driving the car then if I can't remember doing it, I find myself parking on the street in front of the bookstore. I know why I'm here, even if I can't recall the route by which I've arrived. Inside the store, I find the books on the Health wall and take down each of them, their weight in my hands like the soldered ballasts of the balancing man.

"A friend?" Eddie asks, running my total.

"A friend . . . a good friend," I answer, holding the bagged books to my chest.

At the door, I stop and turn, my eyes downcast. "It's not all lyric poetry, Eddie, like you said."

I read into the night, a blanket around my shoulders, Milton purring in my lap. I read the guidelines for safe contact, the controversies over treatments, the demographical statistics. Sunday morning I read more, memorizing the case studies, the health workers' anecdotes, the plethora of pain and sorrow and daily death, and woven through all the words on every page, I read the euphony of devotion. I read about the parents and the partners, the brothers and the sisters, the babies and the children, the lovers. I read as if I'm cramming for a final exam, until my head seems like it will split open with the mass of human distress and superhuman strength, until Milton slaps me with his paw to say enough, get up now, do something.

What I do is take the Buick out after nightfall, when curtains are drawn and street lamps ignited. Here and there someone has forgotten to pull a shade or latch a shutter. I inch the car by these lighted apertures and crane my head to see inside, to envision myself into the frozen vignette: as the woman stirring the cast-iron frying pan on the electric range, as the children grouped about the glimmering light of a television screen, as the angry young man waving a long-necked bottle to an offstage actor. I imagine myself into the lives of these characters who are nothing to me. I rewrite the scenes: the woman turns from the stove to a fistful of daisies in the hand of a husband. The children clamber into the lap of a father, picture books in hand. The young man relents, sits, hangs his head in apology.

At Tryon Street I turn, creeping by the graceful porches, the naked elms. The Leland House is dark except for a second-story window, the window to Austin's study. I stop the car across from the house and watch the glowing glass. What is he doing? Marking papers? Scanning the *Law Review*? Leafing through Dickinson for just the right stanza? Has the book slipped from his hands to the floor? Are his dark eyes closed, is he steeped in thought? Or has he fallen asleep, dreaming? I concentrate absolutely on the panes of glass separating his life from mine. I need to know, if he dreams, of what?

As though I can enter his dreams by force of will, my reverie places me inside the house. I take the polished stairs up to the second floor, push open the study door. I tiptoe to the rocker in which Austin sits and let my hands drop to his shoulders and massage the muscles at the base of his neck.

"That's nice," he says, bending his head back for a kiss.

I kiss him, once on the temple, again on the eyebrow, on the lips.

"Papers done?" I ask, sitting on the floor at his feet.

"Almost."

"Hungry?"

"What have you got?" He lifts my hair, pulls it on top of my head, lets it fall.

"Leftovers? Soup? Canned spaghetti?"

"We don't have canned spaghetti, Dolores."

"I know, sweetheart," I say, resting my head against his knees. We sit, quiet, completed.

We have soup and sandwiches in front of the parlor fire that Austin kindles with trimmings from the wood shop, our plates tabled on our laps. In the kitchen after our simple supper, Austin rinses, I load. I wipe the counter, lifting each of Austin's pill bottles, the alchemy of science and hope that buys us time.

"Coffee?" I ask.

"Not tonight, I don't think."

We climb the stairs to the bedroom, share the bathroom to brush our teeth.

Austin turns on reading lights, and we nestle together under the comforter. I reach for my light, careful of the frame holding the picture of Austin, and turn to wrap my arm across his chest.

"You want lights out?" he says.

"Not yet . . . you read, professor."

Milton jumps on the bed, circles, and beds down in the hollow between our legs.

"Good night, guys," I whisper, yawning.

"Wait for me," Austin says, slipping a bookmark into his text, reaching to his light, cascading the room in sweet darkness, taking me in his arms.

A dog's forlorn howl shears the projection of the tender narrative in my mind, disturbing it with the abruptness of a film gone haywire, the flimsy frames ripped by hasty hands. The study window falls black. The Leland House is immersed in shadow. I pull the Buick from the curb and follow the headlight beams home to the apartment, where I make my bed, the scene I have fashioned an opiate in my veins.

I concoct an anodyne of clandestine appraisals of Austin's days, secret surveys that inch me from imagination to possibility. Sometimes, when the office is slow, I volunteer for the little errands ordinarily assigned to Zoey and drive by the house in daylight, safe from detection in the hours when Austin is teaching. Once, in May's final, sheeting rain, I park the Buick around the corner in front of Trevor Tuskes's and walk the long blocks of Tryon Street. In front of the house I stop and count Aunt Emmabelle's tiger lilies, their strong green palms pushing through the clean earth where months before the unbroken soil appeared upon superficial survey to be wholly barren. I find the new plantings: a Japanese maple uncurling its delicate purple leaves, a trio of birch saplings whose pale bark looks the color of bare skin in the stormy light. Austin has replaced the front doorknob with the housewarming gift from Trevor Tuske; the polished brass gleams, an invitation to enter the unlocked door. Through the beveled glass panes I can see into the parlor where a wingback chair damasked in red roses is drawn close to the fireplace, a newspaper spread over one arm.

Sometimes, if banking or escrows take me out of town, I detour to Davis and circle the campus, drawn to King Hall by the busy clusters of students whose laden backpacks might contain the required textbooks for Austin's courses, or notes from Austin's lectures scratched in student hand, or returned papers marked with Austin's stern, generous comments. I become a sub-rosa parasite on the offshoots of Austin's persisting vitality, hoarding my findings to relish alone in my apartment with Milton as my witness, when I can insinuate myself—a character written in after the fact, an archeologist's wishful salting—into every exhumed detail.

When I do see him, the face behind the wheel of the Jeep, the shadow in the window of the Leland House, my breath catches in my throat and my hand rises to trap the fluttering wings in my heart, thwarting flight the way a birdman might seal his palms around the fight in a broken sparrow to save further damage. Often it comes to me that he senses the secret hours I spend in his life, that I must occupy his thoughts with the same longing which intrudes him into mine. Yet he cannot let me know because I have exiled each of us to separate kingdoms with my cruel decree.

But the kingdom boundaries shift, the crystalline borders wane.

I ask Eddie to order more books. As weeks pass, the table in my kitchenette is covered by Eddie's suggestions, by pamphlets, by newspaper and magazine articles. My research project grows, my ignorance of Austin's disease diminishes. My definition of time expands and contracts and expands again. I look to the cold clinical studies. I look to the tragic first-person remembrances. I look to Dickinson's untitled poems, the intricately knotted lines where horror and ecstasy, dread and delight, death and love, sit beside each other, betrothed in verse after verse after verse.

I weigh the years in my history, the half-life I have accepted with so little question, so much sightless endurance. Against the six months during which Austin and I invented our own physics of time and space, I weigh the whole of my existence. I learn to doubt that paradise refused is protection against paradise lost. And it comes to me, one twilight when sunset shatters the western sky with a glorious gilded challenge to evening, that I would rather live with a transient bliss remembered than a sheltered, sealed contrition.

Every day I check the scales, watching the shifting balance of the suspended trays of lead and gold. Forty lonely years of past time collapses; a future with Austin—five years? fifteen?—extends beyond the horizon.

The trays dip; the gold appreciates.

Jorge has a seventh birthday. We celebrate in the center during the hours of the poetry workshop. I've invited Julian and Lilia and Antonio, Arinda Mesa, Eddie, Zoey and Ted, Dodie and Frank Murphy. The children eat too much strawberry cake and run squealing around the room on sugar highs, midget hooligans celebrating their imminent good luck: a pile of brightly papered gifts tagged with animal cards bearing the names of every student in the workshop. I will give Jorge his true birthday present later, when the other children have gone and Arinda's Spanish will help me explain to Julian how the trust fund works, how it will carry Jorge through four years at Christian Brothers and then on to college, to graduate school if he chooses. Alone, gathering plates and napkins, I think that Austin would have liked this party, that he belonged here with me and Jorge.

I check the scales.

The Volvo's engine is hopeless, the cost of rebuilding the transmission astronomical. I run an ad in the *Daily Democrat* and let it go for two hundred dollars to the best and only offer I get, from the Woodland High machine shop teacher. They built them like tanks in the seventies, he tells me while I clean under the seats and in the trunk, stuffing the detritus of fifteen years into a single paper grocery bag. His kids will spend the year boring holes and setting pistons and slapping Bondo; then the car will be sold to the highest bidder and the profits returned to the shop program. Another civic duty fulfilled.

I check the scales.

Zoey and I close down the office for a week in late April and fly to Seattle for the Northwestern States Realty Convention. Zoey tells me I should attend some of the presentations, that they're not *all* junk. But most of the rain-soaked days I wander the bookstores and drink espresso in the artsy coffeehouses. I stand at the top of the Space Needle, where the view disappoints me and the circular balcony makes me queasy. In our room over commercials during the nightly news, Zoey reads to me her notes on "Customer Satisfaction and the Sales Process: A Two-Way Street"; I put a pillow over my head. We squabble like roommates over which cable movie to watch. On the flight back to Sacramento, Zoey says she feels refreshed, as if she's been on vacation. I feel poised, a balancing woman about to step from the safe center of her lead pedestal onto the golden trail of the rest of her life.

I check the scales.

Every hour I let pass without Austin is one hour I won't have to remember, one hour of the purest gold I cannot shelve in our store of perfect hours. We can make enough of them—these jewels of imperishable memory—we can fill every room of the Leland

House with their resonance so that neither of us lives one moment with regret, ever.

The day comes, a June afternoon, when I understand that I've made a choice, that even though I swooned in despair and fled in ignorance, this match was forged months ago in the deep center of my soul, in the wisdom of my bones. Perhaps my heart has known from the moment I first set eyes on Austin that whatever our destinies, whatever our fortunes, they are meant to be *our* destinies, *our* fortunes.

I will go to the man I love.

I will keep him, and he will keep me, and if the Fates see fit to steal our years or let them run, we will seize our pleasure before it turns to pain.

CHAPTER FIFTEEN

To wait an hour——is long——

To wait an Hour—is long—
If Love be just beyond—
To wait Eternity—is short—
If Love reward the end—

EMILY DICKINSON 1863

ONCE WE ARGUED, Dolores and I, about cutting flowers for the house. She contended that our delight in the presence of cut flowers—the formal yellow glads in a proper vase on the kitchen table, her impulsive spray of red nasturtiums and pink geraniums flourishing in a coffee cup on my desk—warranted the stems severed in the garden beds. A variation of the tree falling in the forest, Austin, she laughed at me. If flowers grow in a garden and the gardener's too absent or too occupied to take pleasure in their beauty, what is their beauty's value? If cut flowers gratify the woman soaping dishes at the sink or pleasure the man seated for hours at his computer keyboard, isn't the value enhanced tenfold? A hedonist's premise, I told her, pulling her to me for a kiss. You could say so, she agreed, her hands locked around my neck.

But hedonism is not the word for the single benefit the doomed man seizes from his terminal sentence: the compulsion to compress thirty years of ecstasy into his allotted final months. In her naive opening statement for the flower defense, Dolores described it as a case for gathering what comes one's way, of making sure nothing is ignored, nothing squandered. You begin to think if you can make it through twenty-four hours without wasting one moment of pure attention, you can stall the wheels of time. You begin to think if you capture every lifting dawn in your memory's eye, every setting sun's orange palette, you can magnify your weeks and months into a lifetime's portion.

When what you have in the present won't satisfy your hunger and you find yourself taunting the boundaries of time by wanting the future—a woman's cool hand laid across your brow, a partner across the linen-draped table whose crystal glass chimes against yours in a toast of thanksgiving—you learn to covet the past. You recall planting a cedar and computing the circumference of its trunk in ten years, twenty, thirty. You remember a sleep-chastened lover in a football jersey who pulls you into her bed at seven in the morning. You picture the woman who is your heart's other half holding a small brown boy in her lap, their heads bent together in conspiracy. You look backward, slake your thirst in the luxury of memory because what you have is what you have today and what you can recall of yesterday. And since one day you will awake and find tomorrow bankrupt, you find yourself rationing even the memories.

You fill your days with diversions.

I join the Labor Department's investigation of the county's agricultural contractors, the focus now not only substandard housing but workplace and transportation violations as well.

I teach a spring semester section of tort law. We approach the sticky issues of compensatory damages and indications of harm, anatomize the high-profile cases stretching the conceivable spectrums of pain and suffering, slide down the slippery slope into the origins of the public's perception of a legal system run amok. I don't have the satisfactory definitive answers to the determinedly raised hands and the sincerely posed questions: whose assessment of pain? Whose analysis of quality of life? Whose determination of loss? Some mornings when my upraised, widespread hands offer my purple scar to the lecture hall to emphasize a point of law and then retreat to a safer pose grasping the lectern for support, I can feel the discussion emigrating from the lucid certainty of law to the equivocal obscurity of philosophy.

My monthly visits to Dr. Hindari have the same inclination to shift fields, and often what begins as a medical exchange concludes as a spiritual one. He schedules my appointments late in the afternoon, and our habit is to talk long past the closing hour, after Carlene has extinguished the lights and locked the clinic's door behind her. He easily dispenses with the indispensable: his deft latex fingers doing their hangman's duty, drawing my blood, and then we sit at our ease over paper cups of coffee or of Coke. I know that ordinarily these tasks of monitoring, of collecting and assessing, would fall to a lab assistant, someone to whom my name connotes nothing but a continuing healthy T-cell count. I appreciate without question that he has become a singular friend, that I seem to be the same to him.

One day, in part spoof and part self-pity, I say that in America my disease has created an untouchable caste, a stratum from which nobody—not white, not educated, not upper class, not male—can elevate. You confess your caste, you make yourself a pariah.

"Look at it another way," Dr. Hindari says gently, shifting his heavy spectacles into place. "Look at it as if you are one of the few who have been given lenses"—he taps his own black frames—"lenses which allow you sight and insight denied to others. . . . Life rarely allows us a training course like the interim between the acquisition of the retrovirus and the onset of disease.

"We consider, in my culture, that a central religious truth comes to us from Shiva's wife. We call her Kali, the goddess of destruction. But we also know her as Parvati, the goddess of motherhood. In Hinduism, she represents to us the incessant movement of time and matter through birth to death."

I listen to his low, even voice, hypnotized by the confirmation his amiable catechism brings my own deductions, my balancing act practiced every day.

"We don't set the two in opposition as does the Western world. They are . . . points on a continuum."

"And my . . . lesson, my certification at the end of this training course . . . ?" I engage with him, the way he intended, the self-pity washed by his cleansing words.

"Ah, Austin, old one," he says, smiling. "You make your way to *moksha*, to the perfection of the soul."

I mull Dr. Hindari's tranquil Hinduism late at night, when I let my mind turn from the immediate and the practical to the metaphysical, when the moon casts the elm trees in shadow against the bedroom ceiling making a maze of light and dark, when I think, always, of Dolores.

I understand—too well, I understand—Dolores's choked explanation to me months ago, the ragged parting, the kind of love that does not equip us for enduring after its breach.

I remember Dolores telling the story of the twin to the Leland House, the mirror image whose pallid apparition I can see on a winter night, the reversed corner tower, the matching gable. We are like the Leland House, she told me once, resting inside the circle of my arms: we make each other whole.

Often, when the house stands still and a century of history seems to share the air I'm breathing, I think I feel her within these walls, by my side. I feel her in the simplest movements: the reach for a glass from a kitchen cupboard, the lift of a log into the firebox, the sweep of a broom across the wooden floor. Mere domestic movements, the labors of husband and wife symbolize the prospect of all that we will lose, the halting ballet before the score ends, before the music runs out.

I drive up Donner Pass on a Saturday morning. On Sunday afternoon, the snowmelt is interrupted by a surprise Alaskan front, and the westbound highway is closed for four hours. I trade a bag of apples for a cup of Thermos chocolate with the young family whose van is wedged behind the Jeep on the highway-turned-snowdrift. The children—younger than six, all three of them—build a snowman beside the Jeep's front bumper. After the snowplows have cleared a lane and we straggle into formation like battle-weary troops, the snowman is tumbled to the pavement and flattened by the trussed tires of the homecoming traffic.

It is well after midnight when I pull the Jeep beside the house. On Monday I lecture through three hours of morning classes, hold a difficult office hour beset by a failing student (no reprieve, I have to tell him: one of advising's sorriest duties), and sit through a two-hour meeting on matriculation demographics and last year's mediocre bar exam pass rates. By late afternoon, when I set my briefcase on the kitchen table and let my jacket drop to the nearest chair, I am too beat to climb the stairs to a real bed. I sit on the love seat, stretch my legs across the battered rosewood coffee table (a donation from Annie's garage once she heard about my wood shop), and rest my head against the carved scrollwork. Fatigue bypasses dreams, and I relax to oblivion, to sleep's barbiturate.

I awaken to a kiss. Not a kiss—a tickle against my cheek, a sandpaper tongue, whiskers, a cat's breath turned to purring, a solid weight warming my chest, unmoving. I touch a head, brush a long tail.

"Not . . . Milton?" I say, squinting in the magicked light showered by the street lamps.

It *is* Milton, there's no doubt when I turn on the reading lamp and stroke his diamond patch. He blinks twice, stretches a paw, and lifts himself from my lap, curious.

"You're a ways from home, Milts," I puzzle.

An incredible journey doesn't make sense; Milton's an apartment cat. He has no reason to know Tryon Street.

Mislaid on a trip to the vet's? Hardly.

Accident?

Coincidence?

The answer comes, the voice from the kitchen, from the country of my heart's cartography.

"He *is* home."

There are points in life, fractures in the channels of ordinary time, when what passes conspires with import so immense that years and years beyond, long into the untold future, remembrance of these points recurs with the same vitality whether it is called on six times a day or six thousand. They hint of immortality, these fractures in time. They are what keep a man alive.

I look up at Dolores, the halo of golden hair, the eyes that see only me.

"I am, too," she says.

Epilogue:
My life closed twice before its close ——

≫

My life closed twice before its close—
It yet remains to see
If Immortality unveil
A third event to me

So huge, so hopeless to conceive
As these that twice befell.
Parting is all we know of heaven,
And all we need of hell.

EMILY DICKINSON 1896

JORGE CALLED TONIGHT, from Children's Hospital in Los Angeles where he is doing his residency. He loves the kids, he says, but despises the city. He is overdosing on fast-food, and he wants me to plant rows and rows of tomatoes so that in August, when he comes home to Woodland, he can eat home-grown tomato sandwiches morning, noon, and night. I pledge that I will plant as soon as the rain stops, and I give him my love.

In my robe, I stand in the kitchen with my hands on the counter. The window over the sink throws back light; I shut off the overhead so that the glass turns from opaque to translucent. The cedar in the backyard bends with the wind; rain pellets against the pane. The seasons speak to me, a gardener now for twenty some springs, with a call that grows more and more insistent every passing year. When the temperature inches upward, when the sun's angle shifts to the north, I worry the garden ahead, turning loam and setting seedlings before anyone else in town. You jump the gun on growing time, Trevor Tuskes used to say: what is it you can't wait for?

I push open the back door and step down to the slate patio. The rain is hard but warm against my skin; it takes only a moment to soak my hair and robe. I kick off my slippers and walk barefoot across the slate to the flower bed where, in my other life, my real life, Austin buried Milton.

In Indian summer, the fall we were forced to abandon our tradition of loading cameras and backpacks and crossing to the east side of the Sierras to see the aspens turn to gold, Milton had curled into the threadbare corner of the love seat and fallen asleep. Gone blind with dignity like the poet whose namesake he became, he lay there without complaint and slipped peacefully from our love. Austin insisted on digging the grave, his arms grown so thin I could see the frightening pull of muscles outlined with every uplifted shovel of the pure dark dirt. Without speaking, we worked together and bedded our old friend into the gentle loam of the Leland House's garden.

A mass of anemones will sprout from the oval swell of ground where he lies. I've never thinned the bulbs; I like to see them multiply, each year thicker and thicker so that every June, something in my throat catches at the vision of the colored carpet of blooms over Milton's little grave.

My Austin has never left me. The Leland House and I are mated to each other now; our lovers welcome phantoms. Zoey asked me, soon after, how I could ever keep living here, how I could bear it. That's just it, Zoe, I told her, it's already over, the hellish part. There is no cup of earth in the gardens his hands haven't worked, no square foot in the Leland House my eyes fall where Austin is absent.

Sometimes, late into night, I can trace his sleeping shadow next to my body, can match the whispered rise and fall of my breath to his.

The remembering doesn't hurt. Every day I relive our heaven; every day toward heaven I draw closer.

Tomorrow, weather willing, I will hurry spring and put down Jorge's tomatoes.